THIS LITTLE THING
CALLED LOVE

UNDER SEATTLE'S SKY SERIES

OTHER BOOKS BY
FRANCES BLACKTHORN

Under Seattle's Sky

Trade Secret of a Messy Relationship
This Little Thing Called Love
Thinking Out Loud

Broken Path

Tainted

THIS LITTLE THING CALLED LOVE

UNDER SEATTLE'S SKY SERIES

FRANCES BLACKTHORN

PROLOGUE

AVA

"You did what?" My voice cracks and the room spins. I'm grappling for reality, "This is a sick joke, right?"

"Ava, babe—" Jax tries.

"Don't 'babe' me, Jax," I hiss, my heart thundering in my chest. "You're telling me, after all the hell we've been through, you just casually slipped into someone else's bed? How can you be so heartless?"

Jax runs a hand through his hair, "It's not like that, Ava. You're getting it all wrong—"

"Wrong?!" I can barely hear my own voice over the blood rushing in my ears. "You think cheating is a matter of interpretation?"

He flinches. "I didn't cheat. You don't understand."

"Then enlighten me, Jax! Make me understand how you're not the villain in this story!" I can feel the tears, hot and angry, threatening to spill.

"Ava, damn it, listen!" Jax's voice rises, matching my own in intensity.

"Fine!" I say, arms folded, ready for whatever lame excuse he's about to throw at me.

Jax steps closer, but I step back, a physical manifestation of the chasm between us. "It was a break, Ava. We were on a break. You left, remember?"

My laughter is bitter, humorless. "Oh, so this is the 'we were on a break' defense? How original. Who are you trying to convince? Me or yourself?"

"You're blowing this way out of proportion and you are being overdramatic. It was just a fling."

"So, I'm 'overdramatic' for being pissed you had a 'fling' weeks after you left New York?"

He sighs, the fight draining out of him. "I thought... I thought we were done. I left, and you also left after that, and I was a mess. It didn't mean anything. Nothing like what you and I have."

I shake my head, "You were a mess? What about me, Jax? Ever thought about how I felt, leaving everything behind, trying to mend a heart you shattered?"

Jax reaches out, but I step out of his reach. "Ava, please. You're the one I want. It was a mistake. A stupid mistake."

"Mistake? Please, Jackson." My voice breaks.

His eyes meet mine, "It's Jax, not Jackson." he corrects me sharply. "I'm a wreck without you, Ava. You know that. I can't lose you over this."

"Fine. Jackson," I emphasize his name, "So let me see if I got this right. You really think I'm overreacting, after you left New York, got cozy with someone else, and then conveniently forgot to mention it when I came back to nurse you post-accident, moved across the country with you, and shared a home for over a year?"

The air is thick with unsaid words. For a moment, we're suspended in time, two broken halves of a once-perfect whole.

"I don't know if I can do this, Jax," I whisper.

"It was just a fucking fling, Ava!"

I raise an eyebrow, my smile twisted with irony. "So, Jax, guess what? Your 'fucking fling' turned out to be a creative collaboration, and voila... she's made a mini you!" I spit out the words, struggling to stay cool. "And the cherry on top? If she hadn't rocked up here in Seattle, baby in tow, playing 'Guess Who's the Daddy?', you'd probably still be playing dumb."

Jax scrambles for words. "Ava, I swear, I had no clue she was pregnant."

"Do you even hear yourself? I mean, can I believe anything you say now?"

"Listen to me, Ava," Jax begs, "Remember who I am. We've been through everything together, way before all this mess."

"JACKSON, YOU'RE A FUCKING DAD!" I explode.

"I DIDN'T KNOW, DAMMIT, AVA!" He roars back, equally loud.

"Fine, let's just... cool it," I say, forcing calmness into my voice. "We've got to sort this out. It's a game-changer."

He nods, trying to seem rational. "Yeah, we'll figure this out. We always do, right?"

But I'm shaking my head, turning away. "No, Jax, this 'we' just became a 'me.' I need space to breathe, to think."

His face is a picture of shock. "You're not serious, Ava..."

I face him, my gaze unflinching. "Dead serious. And tell me, did Rodrigo know about your little escapade?"

"About what? Told you, I was clueless about the pregnancy."

"Not the baby drama, Jax. I'm talking about your secret little rendezvous. That 'fling'."

Jax shakes his head, "Rodrigo? No. We haven't talked much over the years, and when we did our chats never waltz into relationship territory."

"Great. For a moment, I felt like I was the punchline in a cruel joke."

"Babe, let's not jump the gun, okay?" Jax pleads with a desperate edge. "Are we really gonna let some random woman and her claim of a kid blow up everything we've built?"

I let out a harsh, mocking laugh. "Oh, Jax, she's not just 'some random woman.' And that kid? He's got your eyes, your smile."

Jax fires back, "But what if she's spinning a lie?"

I shake my head, disbelief and hurt swirling in my eyes. "Truth or lie, it's not even the point. You kept this hidden, Jax. That's the betrayal."

He raises his voice, "I wasn't unfaithful, Ava! You're painting me as some sort of villain."

"You didn't cheat, but betrayal comes in many forms. And let's not forget, the timeline of this 'fling' conveniently aligns with your New York getaway."

"Would it have changed anything if I'd told you about her then?"

"Really, Jax? You need a roadmap for this?"

"Yeah, Ava, spell it out for me."

"Fine. Flashback to over a year ago. I'm in New York. We rekindle our thing. You had all the time to confess before we jetted off to Seattle. Imagine, I could have been ready for a doorstep surprise featuring your mini-me."

Jax sighs, "You're right. I should've been upfront. I didn't want to hurt you, make things messy. I screwed up, Ava, okay? I'm sorry."

I nod, "I need space, Jax. Time to process."

As I turn to leave, Jax reaches out, but I pull away. "Ava, wait. Can we talk tomorrow? I get it if you need space, but I want to fix this."

His words ring with honesty, but right now, all I can think of is distance. I shake my head gently. "Maybe, Jax. Just... not now."

CHAPTER ONE

AVA

He walks in like he's the king of the world, tall and commanding, oozing confidence that screams 'I own the place.' He doesn't even glance at the reception desk, and that just gets under my skin. I'm on my feet in a flash, my voice sharp as I call out, "Excuse me, sir?" But he acts like I don't even exist. Frustrated, I reach out and tap his shoulder, determined to get his attention.

He spins around, and wow, those amber eyes just knock the wind out of me.

"Hey, you need to sign in first," I throw at him, forcing a polite smile. But this guy, Mr. Too-Good-For-This, doesn't bat an eyelid. His lips might as well be carved from stone. He's a walking, talking embodiment of sharpness and authority, clad in a suit that's as sleek as his attitude.

He barely opens his mouth, as if words are too much effort, then dismisses me with a flick of his hand, his portfolio like an extension of his too-cool-for-school persona.

"Sir, you can't just—" I start to protest, but he's quick to interrupt.

"Yes, I can, love," he says, his voice a mix of British arrogance and a chill that could freeze the Sahara. He looks me over like he's appraising a piece of art, leaving me feeling like I've just been thoroughly evaluated by an expert.

"Listen, I need to record your visit, and possibly assist you. Can we head to the desk?" I try to keep my tone professional, despite the irritation bubbling up inside me.

"I've got it under control," he fires back, his eyes locking onto mine with a force that's almost confrontational. Despite his brusqueness, there's no denying the man is unfairly attractive, with that rugged jawline and meticulously groomed stubble, all topped with light golden-brown hair.

"Excuse me, but I have to inform Mr. Gomez about your arrival. You can't just storm upstairs like–" I attempt again, but he's already talking over me.

Stay calm, Ava.

Breath in. Breath out.

"Rodrigo's an old friend of mine. I'll handle it," and then he's off, striding up the stairs like he owns them.

Rushing back to my desk, I'm dialing Rodrigo as fast as my fingers can move. "Rodrigo, I tried to stop him, but he wouldn't listen," I blurt out, feeling my pulse race.

Rodrigo's response is just a chuckle. "It's all good, Ava. Don't worry about it." He hangs up, and I'm left staring at the phone speechless. Did I just get completely outmaneuvered by a charming Brit and my own boss/friend? It sure seems like it.

—

NICK

"Nicholas Thompson!" Rodrigo's laugh echoes as he slams down the phone, his grin infectious. "Look who decided to grace us with his presence!"

"Rodrigo Gomez," I shoot back, giving him a friendly thump on the back. "Only for you would I brave this chaos."

"It's been ages, man!" He ushers me towards a plush armchair, and I sink in, feeling like I've just stepped into a familiar battleground.

Ditching my blazer, I flash the legal docs. "So, what's the crisis?" I ask, leaning back, ready for the fight.

Rodrigo leans in, "Got a client who's swimming with the IRS sharks. Needs a heavyweight to shield their 'assets,'" he says, his fingers dancing in the air as he quotes.

I raise an eyebrow, "And you thought of me? How flattering."

"You're the tax slayer, Nick. Who else?" Rodrigo says as if I'm the answer to all tax woes.

"Keep buttering me up, Rodrigo. Let's see those details, and I'll weave my magic."

He hands over a piece of paper with the client's info, and I tuck it away. "Good luck, Nick," he says with a wink.

I smirk. "Luck? In my world, it's all skill."

Strutting out of Rodrigo's office, I'm about to dial the client when I'm halted by the receptionist's radiant smile. Ironic, isn't it? After my less-than-stellar entrance.

I take a quick look – those bright blue eyes, the platinum hair – she's like a live wire in this dead zone.

"Nice meeting you, sir," she beams, her dimples adding to her charm.

I nod, keeping it cool, and head for the door. Time to dive into the legal deep end. And as for Ms. Sunshine? *Not today.*

—

"I'm staging an intervention for your client picking skills," I burst into Rodrigo's office, the annoyance from my clash with the British guy still simmering.

"Whoa, slow down!" Rodrigo looks up, his eyebrows doing a little dance of surprise. "What are you even talking about?"

"That British guy!" I snap as if it should be headline news. "He's a one-man wrecking crew for manners!"

"Nick?" Rodrigo's eyebrow arches, a sly grin creeping across his face.

"I don't know his name, but he was an absolute nightmare," I huff, folding my arms tightly.

Rodrigo chuckles, the picture of amusement. "Nick's always been a handful, sure, but he's never been a problem for me. He's... unique."

"Unique? That's a polite way of saying 'nightmare,'" I grumble. "He just marched into the reception area, treated me like part of the furniture, and left with his nose in the air."

Rodrigo bursts out laughing. "Ava, Nick's not some random client. He's an old pal of mine, way back from the pre-New York days."

I pause, processing this new information. Looks like I just got a taste of Rodrigo's 'old friend' charm – British edition.

"Time to audit your friends list, Rodrigo."

He raises an eyebrow, "Planning on including you and Jax in that overhaul, Ava?"

"Well, now that you mention it..." I say, pausing for effect, "Jax is definitely clinching a spot in the dubious zone."

Rodrigo looks puzzled. "Wait, what? Why?"

"Oh, Jax didn't fill you in?" I quip, lacing my words with a heavy dose of sarcasm.

"Fill me in on what, Ava?" Rodrigo leans in, a frown creasing his forehead.

I let out a breath, feeling the weight of my words. "Turns out, Jax is a father."

Rodrigo's eyes widen, "Wait, you're pregnant?"

I almost laugh at the absurdity. "No, Rodrigo. He's already a dad. Not an upcoming one. As in, right now. Not in the future."

He pauses, trying to piece it together. "So, you're saying...?"

"Let me paint the picture," I start, "Jax had a little fun in New York, and surprise – it led to a baby. News to both of us, apparently."

Rodrigo swiftly gets up and shuts the door, his face turning serious. "You mean to tell me Jax has a secret child and kept it from everyone?"

I confirm, "He claims he was clueless about the pregnancy, but never breathed a word about the fling. Then, bam – baby on the doorstep."

Rodrigo looks lost in thought, his expression hardening. "This is a bombshell, Ava..."

"Tell me about it."

Rodrigo's anger is palpable. "I'm going to have a serious talk with Jax. This is unacceptable."

"Rodrigo, stop!" I urge, my emotions spilling over. "I didn't tell you to go off on him. I just needed to vent, to process all this."

He calms down, kneeling to meet my eyes, his hands gently holding mine.

"He has a child, Rodrigo," I whisper, the enormity of it all hitting me. "Everything's changed. And I... I just can't deal with it right now."

I cover my face, trying to hide from the overwhelming wave of feelings.

—

Even after the office clock has called it a day, I'm still camped out at my desk, avoiding the inevitable showdown with Jax. My fingers have been flying over the keyboard, drowning in emails and meeting plans, anything to keep my mind off the mess waiting for me at home.

The sun's long gone, and the office is practically a ghost town when Petra breezes in, hunting for Rodrigo. She's been working at Rodrigo's brother and father's office all day, but it seems like she has come by to join Rodrigo in his journey home.

She clocks my gloomy vibe right away. "Hey, what's up with you?"

I muster up my best fake smile. "Oh, it's all good. Just the usual grind."

"Ava, come on. You're usually the one lighting up this place, but today? You're more like a flickering bulb," she observes, her head cocked in concern.

I exhale a heavy sigh. "I'm just not feeling the whole 'home sweet home' vibe tonight..."

She nods. "Got it. You're still here, and Rodrigo is usually the last one out of the building. That's saying something."

I just shrug, forcing another smile.

Petra extends a comforting hand. "Need to unload? I'm all ears, no judgment."

I shake my head, unable to dive into that emotional pool just yet. "Thanks, Pet, but I can't go there right now."

She gives me a knowing nod. "Fair enough. But if you ever want to spill, just hit me up, okay?" With a blown kiss and a wave, she's off to find Rodrigo.

Later, at my apartment door, I'm rooted to the spot, staring at the white barrier in front of me. My keys jangle against the lock, the door creaking open to reveal Jax, looking up with a smile, and eyes full of concern.

But I'm not in a place to return that warmth. Instead, I step in, drop my keys in my bag, and pull out my phone. My movements are mechanical as I brace for the dreaded talk with Jax, a conversation I've been avoiding all day.

"You're back late," Jax observes.

"Just work stuff," I reply, keeping my gaze fixed on anything but him.

"Have you been avoiding me, Ava?"

I finally meet his eyes. "Yes, Jax, I have been avoiding you," I confess. As he steps closer, I instinctively retreat. "I can't do this right now, Jax. I've been thinking, and... I can't stay here."

"Here? What do you mean?" His voice shakes.

"Here, with you. In this apartment," I say, my voice a hollow echo of its usual self.

"But this is our home," he argues.

"It doesn't feel like 'our' home anymore," I whisper, shutting my eyes to block out the pain.

"Ava..." Jax reaches out, his grip firm on my hand. "Let's talk this through."

I shake my head and pull away, "Talking isn't going to fix this. Think about it, Jax. Were we ever truly at peace here? Since New York, it's been one fight after another. You never wanted Seattle, you just stayed for me. But now, what's a relationship without trust? How can we plan a future on shaky ground?" I pause, my heart heavy. "It feels like we've been against the odds from the start, and now... it's like the universe is confirming it."

Jax's eyes are begging, "But it is right, Ava. I love you. I'm here because I want to be with you."

I shake my head, a bitter laugh escaping my lips. "You're not happy, Jax. Our endless debates about Seattle or New York... and now, with this... how can we move forward?"

"What are you suggesting, Ava? That I just pack up and go back to New York, leave you here, all because you are overreacting about my past?"

"You just don't get it, do you, Jax? For you, it's just a past mistake, it's just an 'overreaction'. But for me, it's a betrayal that cuts deep."

Jax lets out a dry chuckle. "I understand it hurts, Ava. But this can't be the real reason you want to end things. This isn't why you're trying to push me away, back to New York."

"You're missing the point, Jax."

Jax's face hardens, "So, what then? You're just giving up on us? On everything we've built?"

"You're the one who was itching to go back to New York!" I snap.

Jax's voice gains an edge. "But with you, Ava!"

"I'm not going back to New York, Jackson. Not now, not ever!" I shout, letting all my pent-up anger spill out.

Jax's face hardens, a storm brewing in his eyes. "Is this how it ends? You're bailing because of a fling I didn't bring up?"

"For fuck's sake! It wasn't just a fling, Jax!" My voice cracks, "You have a kid. This changes everything! This is a lifetime commitment that I'm not prepared for."

He reaches out, "You don't have to handle it, Ava. This is on me."

"But we're supposed to be a couple, Jax! We're supposed to share our burdens. And I can't shoulder this. I'm only twenty-four. I'm not ready for a child or the responsibility that comes with it."

"You think I planned this? That I wanted to be a father right now?"

"I don't know what goes on in your head, Jax!" I shoot back, "You were the one out there taking risks, not thinking about the consequences!"

His face falls. "So, you want me just to go?"

"I can't be around you, not now," I choke out, feeling my world crumbling. "Take your time to pack up. I'll find somewhere else to stay."

His growl cuts through the tension. "You can't even stand being under the same roof as me?"

"Don't play the victim, Jackson!" I reply, my vision blurred by tears. "Remember the nights you spent on the couch or the nights I cried myself to sleep? Our life here was never the dream we hoped for."

He softens, his voice breaking. "Do you still love me, Ava?"

"I do," I whisper, my heart aching. "But it's different now. It's not the same."

He lets out a harsh laugh, "So, it's deeper than just the child or my solo past. It's about us."

I nod, my sobs growing louder. "Yes, Jax, it's about us. We've hit the breaking point. The child was just the last straw."

He closes the distance, pulling me into a tight embrace. His tears blend with mine as he whispers, "I'm sorry, Ava. God, I'm sorry we ended up here."

Our tears, our shared grief for what we had and what we've lost, fill the room. In his arms, I feel the weight of our broken dreams, the love that's no longer enough to hold us together.

CHAPTER TWO

NICK

Dragging myself into my flat, I shake off the day and the client who's managed to land himself in a mess I'm not even sure I can untangle. All I'm craving now is a stiff drink to wash away the day.

I saunter into the kitchen, dumping my work stuff on the island with a thud that feels oh-so-satisfying. I grab a glass from the dishwasher and when I'm just about to hit up the fridge for something cold my phone starts buzzing like crazy.

Shit, it's Ella.

My phone lights up with her text. "Need you to watch Maggie. Can you?"

"Trouble?"

"I'm out of town for a week, no one to look after Maggie. Can't take her with me," she texts.

Ella, my brother Joshua's wife, and Maggie, their little girl. Joshua's gone, and Ella's all alone in Seattle, family miles away across the ocean in England.

I'm lost in thought, and Ella pings me again. "Nick, please. Maggie loves you. You're the only one I trust."

I exhale, feeling the responsibility settle on my shoulders. "When do you need me?"

"Tomorrow. For a week," she replies.

Great. Just what I needed. I've steered clear of the whole parenting circus for two reasons: no time and, frankly, no partner to go halfsies on a kid with. But if I'm honest, it's mostly about not having a minute to spare.

"Playing nanny now, am I?" I mutter to myself, the irony not lost on me.

"I wouldn't ask if I had another option," Ella's text flashes on my screen. "Leaving her with you in the morning."

I rake a hand through my hair in frustration. "Ella, you do realize babysitting isn't exactly in my daily planner, right?"

Ella's reply buzzes on my phone, "Nick, I'm in a bind. This all came out of nowhere."

I let out a sigh, resigning to the inevitable. "Alright, alright. Just make it at 7 a.m. on the dot. My schedule's squeezed tighter than a rush-hour subway."

—

Come morning, the bell shatters my sleep, yanking me back to reality with its insistent shrieking. Groggily, I grab my phone from the nightstand. 7 a.m. glaring back at me.

"Damn it," I hiss, hauling myself out of bed.

How on earth did I forget the alarm? It's my nightly ritual, my one constant. Looks like today's set to be one of those days.

Halfway to the door, I catch a glimpse of myself in the mirror — *just boxers*. Brilliant. "Oh, it's getting better and better," I grumble, looking down at my striped boxers. Not a chance I'm greeting anyone like this.

I dash back to the bedroom, tearing through my drawers. Salvation comes in the form of grey joggers and a T-shirt. I throw them on in record time, running my fingers through my hair, and swing the door open.

"Uncle Nick!" Maggie, all energy and excitement, crashes into me like a mini whirlwind.

Her enthusiasm's infectious, and I can't help but grin from ear to ear, lifting her into a bear hug. "Hey, Maggs," I say, squeezing her tight. Standing upright with Maggie still in my arms, I shoot Ella an apologetic grin. "Sorry for the delay," I chuckle, "Had a bit of a wardrobe malfunction."

Ella laughs it off. "No worries, Nick."

"So, what's on the agenda today, Ms. Margrett?" I ask, tickling her and eliciting a round of giggles.

"I'm sorry about this. I hate that you have to rearrange your life for Maggie, Nick." Ella says.

I flash Maggie a smile, but inside, I'm gearing up for a storm. "It's all good," I lie smoothly. Truth is, babysitting is a world away from my usual hustle. Full-time kid wrangling? *Not exactly in my skill set.* Maggie's great – a real sweetheart – but let's be real here: playing dad isn't in my cards. My life's a mess as is, and throwing a kiddo into the mix? That's like juggling grenades.

Maggie squirms to get down, so I set her free to explore. I turn back to Ella, my tone dropping. "Look, Ella, I get it, you're in a bind. But let's be clear, this is a one-week deal. After that, I'm out."

Ella's eyes soften. "Josh would have been so proud of you, Nick."

That hits a nerve. "Cut the Josh talk," I snap back, irritation lacing my words. "I'm far from the guy he thought I was. And believe me, I'm no shining example for Maggie."

Ella stands her ground. "That's not true, and you know it. Josh always–"

I cut her off, my voice a low growl. "Stop bringing up Josh. He made his decisions and walked out on his own family. Left Maggie, left you, left all of us. That was his choice."

"He was just chasing his dreams," she murmurs softly.

I shake my head, "Yeah, well, his dreams, his choices, his consequences. Look, Ella, Maggie's great, but she's not my responsibility. I'm only in for a week. That's my limit."

Ella nods, "Okay, one week."

I nod briskly. "Right. Now, if you'll excuse me, I've got work to prep for."

"Of course," Ella responds, her voice warm despite everything. "Thanks again, Nick. You're a lifesaver."

I walk her to the door, where Maggie's already waiting, her little arms wide open for a hug. "Listen to Uncle Nick, okay, Margrett?" Ella says softly, planting a kiss on her forehead.

Ella offers me a grateful smile before stepping out, leaving me standing with Maggie, staring down a week of who knows what.

—

AVA

I'm nursing my morning coffee at my desk, soaking in the rare quiet of an almost deserted office. A few of the IP crew and finance folks are floating around. Rodrigo, though, is MIA. Perks of being the big boss, I guess – roll in whenever you feel like it.

The morning sun is streaming through the massive front windows, painting everything in a golden glow. It's one of those mornings that almost lets you forget the mess of your life. *Almost*. Because, let's be honest, my life's mess has a name, and it's spelled J-A-X.

It's been five whole days since Jax cleared out of the apartment. Couldn't stand the idea of sharing the same space with him, and since the lease is in my name, he was the one to take off. He's probably lounging in some fancy hotel room, delusional enough to think we can salvage whatever's left of us.

I'm lost in the world of emails when suddenly the office door bursts open, a flood of sunlight blinding me for a second. My coffee's halfway to my lips as I prepare for the inevitable interruption.

And in he strides, Mr. British Invasion, making yet another dramatic entry. Just as I was getting comfortable with the idea of a peaceful morning.

This guy's always on a roll, breezing past my desk as if I'm just another piece of office decor. He's all sharp in a sleek black suit and white shirt, sporting sunglasses like he's about to hit a movie set. No hellos, no small talk, just beelines straight for the stairs as if he's got a secret rendezvous with royalty. And there goes my quiet morning – just another typical day at the office.

I stride away from my desk, smoothing down my dress, ready to get a word with this mystery man – Nick, if I recall correctly.

As I approach the stairs, there he is, Nick, coming down like he's the king of the castle. He halts, those sunglasses still glued to his face. "Where's Rodrigo?" he demands, cutting right to the chase.

"First," I say, mustering up my politest smile. "Good morning to you too, sir," His reaction's hidden behind those dark lenses, but I press on. "Second, Rodrigo's not in yet."

About to deliver my next point, he breezes past me.

I'm momentarily thrown but quickly regain my footing. "I wasn't done – third!"

Nick pauses, finally ditching the sunglasses. He gives me this blank look, slightly cocking his head.

"Third," I continue, "You can't just strut in here like you run the show."

He's silent for a beat, then hits me with, "Love, do you even know who you're talking to?"

I stand my ground, still smiling. "No, sir, I don't. And respectfully, I don't really care."

He looks at me for some time in silence before saying, "Well, when Rodrigo shows up, tell him Nick stopped by. It's important."

And with that, he spins on his heel and strides off.

Who in the world does this guy think he is?

—

NICK
MINUTES BEFORE

Just as I'm strapping Maggie into the car, ready for our day out, my phone erupts into a chorus of rings. Great, it's the client Rodrigo dumped on me.

"Morning, how can I help?" I say, phone wedged between my cheek and shoulder, while I'm wrestling with Maggie's seatbelt.

"I need to see you today. This morning, if possible," the client demands.

Fantastic. With Maggie in tow, and an office to get to, this is just what I needed.

Can I leave Maggie alone for a bit in my office while I meet this guy?

No... you can't Nicholas.

"Alright, how about my office at 10?" I suggest, trying to keep it together.

"No, can you come to our place? We've got a team who needs to talk to you too," he replies.

I close my eyes, muttering a silent, "Damn my life." I secure Maggie in, phone still clutched in hand. "Fine, send me the address. I'll be there."

"Perfect, thanks, Mr. Thompson," he says, sounding way too happy for my liking.

"Sure thing," I reply, a bit miffed. Call done, I head to the driver's side, grumbling under my breath, "Welcome to the Nick and Maggie circus."

Driving away, I'm at a total loss. The past few days have been smooth sailing – clients came to me, Maggie chilled with Hannah, my receptionist. But today? *Today wasn't part of my plans*. Hannah's off, and I can't drag Maggie to a client meeting.

Then it hits me. Rodrigo Gomez. Good old Rod, who got me into this mess, can surely spare a couple of hours for Maggie. *No sweat*.

I shift gears and zoom towards Rodrigo's office. "Won't be long, Maggs," I tell her, her smile making her look like a little cherub.

I burst out of the car and sprint into the building, not giving anyone a second glance. Time's ticking. I rush up to Rodrigo's office, burst in, ready to plead, "Rod...", but the place is empty. Just my luck.

As I spin around to leave, there she is – the stunning blonde from before. I take a moment to appreciate the way her light blue dress complements her features. But then, I snap back to reality, thankful for my shades hiding my obvious once-over. No need for her to catch me ogling.

"Where's Rodrigo?" I ask her.

She hits me with a bright smile. "First, good morning to you too, sir." I take a quick glance at her dress before she goes on, "Second, Rodrigo's not in yet."

She's about to say something else, but I've got zero time for small talk. I've got Maggie in the car and a world of trouble waiting.

"I wasn't done – third!" she calls out, her voice surprisingly strong. It stops me in my tracks. I slide off my shades, giving her my full attention. "Third," she continues, visibly gathering her thoughts, "You can't just strut in here like you run the show."

I take a beat to consider her words. "Love, do you even know who you're talking to?"

I am amused. Who is this girl?

"No, sir, I don't. And respectfully, I don't really care." she says, her tone polite as she smiles. This girl's got guts, I'll give her that. A polite spitfire.

A grin almost breaks across my face, "Well, when Rodrigo shows up, tell him Nick stopped by. It's important." With that, I turn on my heel and head out.

CHAPTER THREE

AVA

Rodrigo walks in, looking all boss-like, with Nick in tow. And guess who's trailing behind them? Petra, gripping the hand of this little munchkin. She's tiny, maybe four or five years old.

I sneak a quick glance at Nick and then at the kid. Holy resemblance! Mr. Mysterious has a mini-me. Great, what is it with men and surprise kiddos lately? Is this some new trend I missed the memo on?

"Morning, Ava," Rodrigo says, giving my desk a friendly tap before heading upstairs with Mr. Daddy Cool. Petra sidles over with a big smile.

"Isn't she the cutest?" she gushes.

Not gonna lie, the kid's a cutie – all light brown hair and big amber eyes. "She's adorable, but kids are kind of a sore spot right now," I admit with a forced smile.

Petra leans in. "Still rough waters with Jax, huh?"

I nod. "Yep. He's holed up in some hotel, dreaming we'll rewind and replay."

She nudges me. "So, you're done-done?"

"Pet, between you and me," I start in a hush, "I think I'm over Jax. The whole baby mama drama was just the universe telling me to cut loose. Time for Ava to fly solo."

Petra nods, "You gotta do what makes you happy, Ava. Even Rodrigo gets that, though he's Mr. Tight-Lipped about feelings.

And trust me, he's bummed, but he's not picking sides. If you're not happy with Jax, then it's best to be alone or with someone else "

"Thanks, but I'm off the dating market. Ava's taking a love vacation." I glance at the little girl. "So, what's the story with the pint-sized guest?"

"Nicholas needs a babysitter for the kiddo for an hour while he's at a meeting." Petra fills me in.

"What are we now, the office daycare?" My joke earns a chuckle from Petra.

"Hardly. There's this client who's got Nick running around, insisted on him being at their place for a meeting. And well, dragging a kid along wasn't an option. Since Rodrigo's the one who linked them up, he's pitching in to help out Nick. It's just for a bit."

Petra's about to spill more tea, but then Rodrigo and Nick strut back in, and she clams up with a knowing smile. Nick shoots her a grin that vanishes the second he looks my way.

He crouches down to the little girl's level. "Maggie, be a star with my mates here, okay?" He's met with a bear hug from the tot.

"Where you going?" she pipes up, her British accent tugging at my heartstrings.

"Just a quick work thing. I'll be back before you miss me," Nick reassures her, planting a kiss on her forehead. Standing, he clasps Rodrigo's hand, only to get yanked into a bro hug, mumbling a "Cheers, mate," before ducking out of the office.

———

An hour flies by, and here comes Rodrigo, little Maggie in tow. "Ava," he says, a hint of apology in his voice. "Nick's meeting's turned into a saga. He needs us to watch Maggie a bit longer. I've got a meeting now, and Petra's heading out."

I arch an eyebrow at the cute munchkin. "So, you're dropping off this little cutie with me?" I flash her a smile, and she giggles.

Rodrigo rubs the back of his neck. "Yeah, sorry about this. Can't have her in my office, and Petra's got to go."

"No problem," I assure him. "We'll hang out for a bit."

Rodrigo leans in and plants a grateful kiss on my forehead. "You're a lifesaver, Ava."

"Sure, sure."

Petra dashes down the stairs, pecks Rodrigo on the cheek, ruffles Maggie's hair, and shoots me a wink. "Gotta split to the other office. Back after lunch!"

I nod at Petra and move around the desk to grab Maggie's hand. Rodrigo flashes me a grateful smile and heads upstairs, hollering, "Send up any clients that arrive, will ya?"

"Got it, boss," I call back, crouching next to Maggie and being extra careful with my dress.

"You so pretty," Maggie blurts out, beaming at me.

I chuckle. "Thanks. You're quite the princess yourself." Taking her hand, I lead her to my side of the desk, setting up camp for our little impromptu hangout.

Another hour ticks by, and there's still no sign of Nick. I'm starting to feel the pressure. Maggie's been on repeat about being hungry, and Rodrigo's tied up in back-to-back meetings. Lunchtime's creeping up on me, and my stomach's growling.

What's a girl to do?

I know barging into Rodrigo's meetings is a no-go, but I'm in a bind here. I grab the reception phone and dial his office.

"Ava?" Rodrigo's voice comes through.

"Hey, so Nick's still nowhere to be seen, and I'm supposed to be on my lunch break. Maggie's starving. Is it cool if I take her out for a bite?" I rush out the words. "Sorry to bug you, just didn't want to jet off without the green light."

Rodrigo lets out a soft laugh. "Go ahead. If Nick shows up, I'll fill him in."

"Thanks Rod," I say, hanging up. I turn to Maggie with a grin. "Ready for a lunch adventure?"

Her face lights up, and she hops off the chair, grabbing my hand. "Yes!"

I scoop up my white flap bag, slip my phone inside, and make it secure. Hand in hand with Maggie, I give the office crowd a quick heads-up. "Off to lunch, people!"

Me and Maggie are strolling down the street when I decide to start a conversation.

"So, what are you in the mood for, food-wise?"

Her face lights up. "Pizza!"

"That's what I'm talking about!" I say, giving her hand a little squeeze. "Got a favorite kind?"

She beams. "Margherita!"

"Why Margherita?"

"Sounds like my name – Margrett!" she says, giggling.

"Got it, Margrett Pizza it is," I joke, guiding us to a pizza place just around the corner from the office.

The pizza place is nice and mellow – just what we need. I order up a medium Margherita pizza, thinking it's probably more than enough for little Maggie and me.

"So, how old are you now, Maggie?" I ask as we settle in.

She proudly holds up four fingers.

"Four," I confirm, and she nods vigorously. "That's a pretty big number," I say, playing along. "You're getting all grown up."

"How old are you?" She flips the question back to me.

"I'm twenty-four," I chuckle. "Way older than you."

"Wow," she giggles. "Uncle Nick's older too."

Hold up – Uncle Nick? So, Maggie's not his daughter, she's his niece. That's new to me.

"Yeah, Uncle Nick's probably a bit older than me," I play along.

She pauses, counting on her fingers, then shows me six. "He's three-three!"

"You're a smart cookie, Maggie." I give her a warm smile.

Then the pizza lands on our table, and Maggie's face is pure gold. She tackles her slice like it's her job.

"It's good, right?" I say, taking a bite.

She nods enthusiastically. "Told you it was my favorite!"

We talk about everything – her favorite color, her dream of being a 'vet-anarian'. It's pretty darn cute.

By the time we finish up, I realize how much I needed this little break. Maggie's a total ray of sunshine.

"Ready to head back?" I ask, scooping up the bill. She's all nods and smiles, so off we go, back to the grind.

—

NICK

I try ringing Rodrigo, but no dice.

"Bummer, the meeting's gone longer than I thought."

In a flash, I pull up at the building and hustle inside. The reception is empty, but then this young lady comes up, giving me the scoop, "Ava's grabbed lunch with the little one, and Rodrigo's tied up in a meeting." Ava – that's the name. The girl who's all sunshine and smiles. Fits her like a glove.

I just nod and step back outside, taking a second to breathe.

Off in the distance, there's Maggie, bouncing around like she's on springs, all laughter and joy, with Ava right beside her. Ava's looking... well, she's looking stunning, and there's a smile that creeps onto my face. *Damn it...* Something about this girl screams 'trouble', and I've got a soft spot for trouble.

"Uncle Nick!" Maggie spots me and bolts, leaving Ava behind as she zooms my way.

"Hello there, young miss," I say, scooping Maggie up. "Rule number one: never let go of someone's hand when you're out and about, got it?"

She bats her lashes at me. "But I missed you," she says, all doe-eyed.

"Missed me or not, you can't go running off like that. Your mum would have my head," I tell her, half-joking, but mostly serious.

Maggie nods, all serious now, then suddenly lights up. "Ava and I had pizza!"

I glance at Ava, who's giving a casual wave. "Oh yeah?" I ask Maggie.

"Margrett's pizza!" she beams.

Ava's laugh is infectious, and Maggie's giggling along. I try to keep a straight face. "That's it, young lady. No more fast food."

Ava looks a bit sheepish. "I didn't mean to, just didn't know what else to get her. She was hungry–"

"It's alright."

"But Uncle Nick," Maggie chimes in, "That pizza wasn't fast food."

"Oh? Do tell," I ask.

"It took ages to come! That's not fast," she explains, and that sets blondie and me off laughing.

I stroll back into the building and head upstairs to thank Rodrigo for playing uncle to Maggie. "You're a lifesaver, mate. Would've been in a right mess without your help."

"It was actually Ava who stepped up," Rodrigo corrects me. "I was swamped with meetings, Petra was out, and Ava jumped in to save the day."

"The sunshine girl?"

Rodrigo chuckles, "She's practically a human sunbeam. But heads up, I don't think she's your biggest fan."

I laugh. "Yeah, I kinda got that. She say anything about me?"

"Oh, she did. She had a few choice words after you stormed in here. Something about my needing to upgrade my client list... You sure left a mark."

"I'll chalk that up to my irresistible charm," I joke.

"Or your knack for being a grump," Rodrigo shoots back.

"Fun as this is, I've got to run. Time to collect Maggie and hit the road," I say, "Thanks a bunch."

"No worries, pal," Rodrigo replies, his British accent imitation making me shake my head and smirk as I head out.

Downstairs, I spot Maggie, clinging to Ava like she's her personal hero, deep in conversation with a client. Only from here can I see her behind the desk.

Ava shoots a quick look my way before diving back into her conversation. I lean on the desk, peering over to give Maggie a little grin. She giggles, but doesn't budge from Ava's side.

"Absolutely, sir," Ava's saying to the client. "I'll relay your message to Mr. Gomez and sort out those meeting dates for you." She beams at the client who then departs.

"Looks like I owe you, sunshine," I say to Ava, catching her off guard.

She's about to say something, but I'm already crouching down by Maggie. I sneak a quick look at Ava's legs – *whoa, easy there, Nicholas*. I snap back to the moment and focus on Maggie. "Ready to roll, Maggs?"

She shakes her head, her grip on Ava unyielding. "I wanna stay with Ava. I like her."

Well, that settles it. Maggie's made her choice.

Ava gently pats Maggie's hair. "I've got work, sweetie, and so does Uncle Nick. You gotta go with him, okay?" Hearing her call me 'Uncle Nick' is definitely something else.

Maggie's bottom lip quivers. "But I wanna stay with Ava."

"Am I chopped liver to you now?" I tease her, putting on a serious face.

"I wanna be with both!" she sniffles.

"That's a bit tricky, kiddo," I chuckle.

Ava jumps in, smoothing Maggie's hair. "Let's make a deal, yeah? Next time Uncle Nick is free, we'll all do something fun. How's that sound?"

Maggie nods, her tears easing up. Ava's idea catches me off guard. *What's is she even doing?*

I sneak a peek at Ava and, yep, my eyes linger a bit too long on her legs – *again*. She's quick to call me out, "Eyes up here, Mr. Nicholas."

"It's Thompson, actually. Nicholas Thompson," I correct her, trying to look dignified.

She fires back, "Apologies, Mr. Thompson. But that doesn't give you a free pass to stare at my legs."

"Fair point, Ms....?" I leave it hanging.

"Adams," she fills in, still giving me the teacher look.

"Ms. Adams, Ava Adams," I say. "Won't happen again."

Just then, Maggie tugs at my hand, pulling me back to reality. "Uncle Nick, are we seeing Hannah now?"

"Nah, Maggs, we're heading to my office. Hannah's out today."

Petra pops up behind us, "Is Rodrigo out of his meeting?"

"Yeah, he's back in his office," Ava says, all smiles.

Petra tosses a cheeky grin my way. "Handled the demanding client Rodrigo sent your way?"

I chuckle. "Oh, he's been a real peach. Come on, Maggie, let's get going." I offer my hand, and she's quick to take it. Time to make our exit.

CHAPTER FOUR

AVA

"Alright, give me the dirt," Petra says, her eyes gleaming with mischief once Nick and Maggie are gone.

"Dirt on what?"

"Don't play innocent, Ava," she chides with a teasing smile. "You and Nicholas Thompson? The sparks were practically flying."

"Please, Petra. The guy's as warm as an iceberg."

She waves me off. "Oh, come on. The way he was checking you out? He looked like he wanted to eat you up."

"Petra!" I gasp, "No way. Plus, pretty sure he's taken!"

She arches an eyebrow. "He's got a girlfriend, and he's eyeing you like that? Ouch for her." Petra breaks into laughter.

"Maggie mentioned her. Some girl named Hannah."

"Yeah, yeah. Whatever you say." She flounces off upstairs, leaving me to mull over the ridiculous idea of Nick looking at me like that. To him, I'm pretty sure I'm just part of the office decor.

———

The office is practically a ghost town now, with just the usual suspects – me, Rodrigo, and Petra – still hanging around upstairs. I power down my computer, get my bag and cardigan, and head up to say my goodbyes. I tap on Rodrigo's door and poke my head in. "Catch you tomorrow."

"Night, Ava," Rodrigo calls back, while Petra chimes in with a cheerful "Bye, Ava!"

Stepping out into the night, the cool air hits me like a wake-up call. I stride over to my white rover, the city lights twinkling like distant stars, the buzz of traffic playing its own kind of lullaby.

Back at my place, I go through the usual drill – drop the bag, ditch the shoes, and slip into the kitchen in my comfy blue socks. Time for my post-work unwind ritual: a cup of soothing rooibos tea. I settle at my kitchen island, painted a calming sage green, sipping away the day's chaos. Then, of course, my phone decides to crash the party, blaring from inside my bag by the door.

"Of course," I mutter, forgetting I'd left it there. Typical end to a typical day.

I let out a sigh and grab my phone.

And, of course, it's Jax on the line. I pause, then decide to answer, "Hey."

"I need to talk. Can I come by?" he asks.

"I dunno, Jax..."

"Come on, Ava. Can't say it over the phone."

"Tonight?"

"Yeah, tonight, please." he replies.

I give in. "Okay, come over."

Not ten minutes later, there's a ring at the door. Jax, as expected. He gives me a quick, polite peck on the cheek and steps inside.

"So, what's the big news?" I ask, leaning against the door, curious but cautious.

"I'm moving back to New York."

His words hit me like a ton of bricks. I mean, I saw it coming, but still. "Okay," is all I manage, my heart sinking.

"Are you okay with that?" he asks, stepping closer.

"Yeah, just trying to process it all," I offer him a weak smile.

"You did suggest it, remember?" he points out.

"I did," I wrap my arms around myself. "But it's different actually hearing you say it."

"I love you." He says, gently caressing my cheek.

I whisper back, "I love you too."

"I know you do, but it's just not the right kind of love," he says, heavy-hearted.

"When are you leaving?"

"Tomorrow. I had to tell you face-to-face."

"And the kid? That woman?"

"They're coming with me," he replies. "If the kid really is mine, I have to do the right thing."

Tears start to well up in my eyes. *This is really happening.*

Jax pulls me close, whispering, "Let it out, Ava."

So, in the dim hallway, I let go, tears streaming down my face.

—

NICK

I'm lounging on the couch, just staring at the ceiling. Maggie's out like a light in my bed, and all I've got on my brain is Ava – the sunshine girl. Every time she crosses my mind, there's this buzz, like I'm hooked up to some kind of live wire.

Her laugh, that smile, her voice... *get a grip, Nick.*

She's got this aura of kindness. Like she's genuinely good to the core, and man, is she easy on the eyes. Complete opposite of yours truly – *minus the easy on the eyes part*. And yet, here I am, totally hung up on a girl I barely know.

I've always been Mr. Casual, never one for the long haul. And I'm not about to flip the script for Ava – it's only been a couple of brief run-ins, after all. But something about her, that sparkle in her smile, has got me tied up in knots.

Making a move would be easy, though. She's nice, seems to like my niece, works with Rodrigo – the path's clear. Chasing her just because she's got that charm and is within arm's reach? That's not my style. Plus, I don't want to mess things up – *for either of us*.

"Snap out of it!" I tell myself, loud enough to break the silence. "Pull it together, Nicholas George Thompson." I mutter.

Dragging myself up, I head to the kitchen. The fridge offers nothing tempting, so I make my way for the mini bar and pour a bourbon.

Maybe this'll straighten out my head.

Out on the balcony, bourbon in hand, I let the night air cool me down.

Next morning, my alarm's blaring, and my head's pounding – note to self: bourbon and waking up early don't mix. Groaning, I get up to wake Maggie. "Rise and shine, Maggs," I say softly, watching her stretch.

I splash water on my face, then head for a shower, letting the hot water try to scrub away both the hangover and thoughts of Ms. Sunshine.

But it's a lost cause – she's still there, front and center in my mind, refusing to be drowned out by last night's bourbon.

"Uncle Nick!" Maggie bursts into the bathroom, catching me totally off guard in the shower.

Snatching a towel from the door, I hastily cover up. "Whoa, Margrett! Man's showering here! You can't just storm in!"

"But Mum lets me," she says innocently.

"Yeah, well, that's Mum," I grumble. "For heaven's sake, Maggie, turn around!"

She spins around, but now she's crying.

"Just perfect," I mutter to myself.

I wrap up the shower quickly and get dressed, feeling guilty for making her cry. In my room, I find Maggie on the bed, tears streaking her face.

"Hey, I'm sorry for yelling," I say, sitting beside her and pulling her into a hug. "Took me by surprise, that's all. We good?"

She nods, sniffling. "I'm sorry for barging in, Uncle Nick."

I smile. "All's forgiven. How about we kick off the day with breakfast?" I tousle her hair playfully. "And did I hear 'barging' from you? That's a big word!"

She grins, taking my hand. "I'm very clever, you know."

"Sure are, little one."

—

Driving to the office, Maggie suddenly hits me with, "Did you know Ava is twenty-four?" I almost choke on my spit.

What is this? Is Maggie moonlighting as a pint-sized secret agent?

"Really?" I play along, trying to sound casual.

"Yeah," she giggles, "I told her you're three-three!"

"You did, huh?" I glance at her, "Nice of you to share that, Maggs."

"Yeah, Uncle Nick," she beams, proud as a peacock.

"Did she react to that bit of news?"

Maggie shrugs. "I dunno." Of course, she wouldn't notice. What am I even thinking? Why would a four-year-old care about age surprises?

I turn my attention back to the road, but it's not long before Maggie pipes up again. "Can we see Ava again today, Uncle Nick?"

I hesitate, "Well, Ava's got work today. And so do I. Maybe some other time, okay?"

"But yesterday you were working, and so was Ava, and I was still with her," Maggie counters, hitting me with some solid kid logic.

I can't argue with that. "True, but yesterday was a bit different, Maggs. Ava knew you were coming. Today, not so much."

"She doesn't want to see me?" The way she looks at me, those big, innocent eyes... I quickly glance at her.

"Of course, she does. Ava had a blast with you," I reassure her.

"So, we can go see her?" She's practically bouncing in her seat.

I let out a sigh. "Not today, kiddo."

"We could call her, let her know we're coming?" she suggests, ever hopeful.

"I don't have her number."

"Just ask Rodrigo then," she's not giving up.

"Maggie, you're too clever for your own good. But no, it's not that simple."

"Don't you guys talk?" she probes further.

"Why do you ask?"

"Friends have each other's phone numbers," she states matter-of-factly.

I shake my head. "Well, I guess you're better friends with Ava than I am."

She pauses, then says, "I like Ava."

"I know you do," I smile, glancing at her in the rearview mirror. "And I'm sure she likes you too, Maggs."

AVA

Heading out of the office, I'm undecided about lunch, my mind still replaying last night's chat with Jax about his New York move. *My appetite's taken a hit.*

"Ms. Adams," a familiar British accent interrupts my thoughts. Nick, looking sharp as ever in a grey suit and white shirt, coolly sporting sunglasses and holding Maggie's hand.

"Mr. Thompson," I say, matching his formality but managing a smile, unlike his serious expression. Crouching to hug Maggie, she dashes into my arms. "You look so pretty in yellow," she beams, eyeing my dress.

"Thank you, darling. You look so pretty as well," I return the compliment, catching a rare smile from Nick.

"Maggs insisted on visiting," Nick says.

I look at Maggie. "Really?"

"Yep, I missed you, Ava!" she admits.

"Missed you too, little one." I say, giving her a smile.

Maggie's eyes light up. "Can we have lunch like yesterday?"

Nick jumps in, cautioning Maggie, "Hold on, speedy bean..." He gently taps her shoulder. "Ava's got work, you know. You can't hog her all day. Nice to see her, but now we've got to scoot."

Maggie's face falls, tears threatening to spill. "But I wanna stay with Ava..."

I catch Nick's eye. "I am on my lunch break. If it's okay with you, I totally don't mind having lunch with her." I offer.

"With us," he clarifies, eyes locked on mine.

I hesitate, then say, "Sure, both of you."

Maggie's tears vanish as quickly as they came, replaced by a huge smile. But Nick's quick to temper her excitement. "I didn't confirm we're having lunch with Ava..."

Maggie's lip quivers again. I give Nick a pleading look, silently mouthing, "Please?"

He sighs, relenting. "Alright, fine."

Maggie's over the moon, hugging my legs, making my braid dance along. I laugh, genuinely happy.

Nick strides past, asking, "So, where to for lunch?"

"PIZZA!" Maggie shouts.

Nick shakes his head. "No pizza today, Maggs."

I jump in, backing him up. "I'm with Uncle Nick on this. How about we pick something else? What do you think, Uncle Nick?" I tease, laying it on thick with his name. Maggie looks to him expectantly.

Nick's face remains a mystery, no hint of a smile. "Ava's call."

"How about pasta?" I suggest.

Maggie cheers, easily swayed.

"Pasta it is," Nick agrees, still poker-faced.

We head off to a nearby Italian spot, Maggie bouncing between us, humming a tune, gripping our hands.

Lunch with Nick and Maggie turns into an impromptu spaghetti show, with Maggie as the star performer.

"She's really digging in," I comment, watching her tackle her pasta with gusto.

Nick chuckles, a sound that's surprisingly warm. "She's got a knack for it."

I decide to test the waters a bit. "You know, she's got your look. It's pretty uncanny."

He meets my gaze, and there's a flicker of something deep in those amber eyes. "She's my niece," he says. "Got the Thompson genes."

"So, she's from your brother or sister's side?" I ask, genuinely curious.

He opens his mouth to answer, but Maggie interrupts with a sauce-covered smile. "I'm Daddy's girl!" she declares proudly.

I laugh, reaching over to wipe her face. "You sure are, sweetie."

Nick shifts his gaze away, and Maggie's next words tug at my heartstrings. "Daddy's not here anymore. But I've got Uncle Nick and Mum."

The look on Nick's face is unreadable, "Well, you're lucky to have them," I say, gently patting her hand.

I steal glances at Nick, waiting for him to meet my eyes, but he doesn't. "More juice, Maggs?" he asks, breaking the silence. She nods, and he signals the waiter.

Then, out of nowhere, Maggie perks up. "Ava, wanna hear something funny?"

Nick's giving Maggie that 'be-careful-what-you-say' look, but I'm all in for whatever tale she's about to spin. "I'd love to hear your story, Maggie."

Maggie, unfazed by Nick's glare, starts, "This morning, I went to the bathroom and–"

Nick cuts in, leaning forward and snapping his fingers. "Whoa, hold up! No need to share that story, Maggs."

Maggie pouts, her little face scrunching up. "But it's a good story!"

Nick holds firm, though there's a twinkle in his eye. "Trust me, it's not for public consumption."

"Now you've piqued my curiosity," I admit.

"Believe me, you're better off not knowing." Nick says not looking at me.

Maggie, not one to be silenced, blurts out with a giggle, "Uncle Nick was all naked when I ran into the bathroom while he was showering!"

I choke on my drink, trying to contain my laughter. Maggie's sitting there, triumphant and pleased as punch with herself.

Nick throws me an amused glance. "Really helping the situation there, Ava." he chuckles, trying to maintain some semblance of seriousness.

I'm trying to compose myself, but it's hard. "Sorry, it's just... that's classic kid oversharing!"

Nick shakes his head, but he's definitely fighting back a smile. "You two are a pair. Can't take my eyes off you for a second."

I wipe away a tear from laughing so hard.

Nick leans back, crossing his arms.

Maggie beams, pleased with the chaos she's caused. "Uncle Nick's funny when he is embarrassed!"

He playfully scolds her, "You're walking a fine line, young lady. We're gonna have to talk about this later."

Unbothered, Maggie lets out a peal of laughter. "I think Ava likes your smiles, Uncle Nick!"

I raise an eyebrow, "Does she now?"

"Be careful, sunshine. You keep this up, you'll be the star of Maggie's next big story."

—

NICK

Ava's laughter is something else, *I swear*. It's got this pull on me that I just can't shake off. Never really craved anyone's attention, but hers? It's a whole different story.

Unsettling? Definitely. But somehow, I'm drawn to it like a moth to a flame.

"Ava, did you know Uncle Nick rides motorbikes?" Maggie says it out of nowhere. This girl.

I try to nudge the conversation elsewhere. "Maggie, I doubt Ava's all that interested in my biking habits," I say, hoping she'll drop it.

"Actually, I'm quite curious about that," Ava admits, her head cocked in that cute way of hers.

Our eyes lock, and I can't help but respond with a bit of a tease. "Really? Never pictured you as the motorbike type." I'm struggling to keep my face straight, a smirk threatening to break through.

Ava's eyebrows shoot up, a sly smile playing on her lips. "Looks like you're quick to judge, Mr. Thompson."

"Not judging, just an observation," I argue, enjoying this back-and-forth more than I should.

"Is it the dress or the braid?" she asks, her eyes sealed on mine. I can feel my heartbeat pick up, and there's a part of me that's itching to rise to her challenge, but I play it safe and turn to Maggie for a distraction.

Then Maggie, bless her heart, innocently suggests, "You should join us on a motorbike ride, Ava!" I try to send her a silent 'no' with a wide-eyed look, but Maggie's too wrapped up in her own excitement.

"Sorry, Maggs, Ava's missing the requisite black leather pants for bike rides."

Quick as a flash, Ava says, "Actually, I have a pair of leather trousers, ready for any adventure." Her boldness takes me by surprise, and I find myself momentarily lost for words.

Maggie's ecstatic. "See, Uncle Nick! Ava can come!"

"Might need to rethink my riding rules," I say.

Then Maggie throws another question into the mix. "Do you swim, Ava? Can you swim?"

I give Maggie a quick, warning glance, hoping she'll drop it, but Ava jumps in. "Nope, I can't swim," she admits, her gaze shifting shyly to Maggie.

Maggie's eyes widen. "You don't? But I do!"

Ava plays into her excitement. "Really? That's incredible! You must be very talented."

Maggie beams, pride swelling in her voice. "My daddy taught me. He was a really good swimmer." I can feel a knot forming in my stomach at the mention of her dad.

Sensing my discomfort, Ava smoothly diverts the conversation. "Swimming's cool, but you know what I'm really good at?"

Maggie leans forward, "What can you do?"

"I play the piano," Ava reveals with a glint in her eye. I can already tell this is going to spiral into a long, drawn-out conversation.

"Show me!" Maggie's eyes light up, practically sparkling.

I jump in, "Maggie, have you finished your pasta?"

Ava chuckles. "My piano's back in New York. I haven't got one here in Seattle."

She's a New Yorker? That's news to me.

Maggie, ever the informer, pipes up, "But Uncle Nick has a piano!"

Ava gives me a quick, knowing smile. "Really now?"

I cough awkwardly. "Yeah, I do."

Ava's curiosity is piqued. "Do you play?"

But Maggie's already ahead of us. "Uncle Nick plays guitar too! At a bar!" Her excitement is through the roof.

I raise an eyebrow. "That's right. But that bar's no place for kids."

Ava leans in, "Why's that?"

I put on a serious face. "It's... let's just say it's not the most refined place. Think rowdy crowds and smoke thick enough to cut with a knife."

Ava grins. "Sounds like my kind of scene."

I let a smile escape. "You might just fit right in."

Maggie's all excited. "Can I go see you play?"

"Not just yet, Maggs," I shake my head. "Bars aren't for little ones."

Maggie pouts. "I've never been to a bar. Uncle Nick and Mum always say no."

I give her a smile. "One day, when you're old enough, I'll take you to see a show, promise."

"When are you playing again?" Ava asks.

I pause, weighing whether to tell her or not. "Actually, I'm playing tonight."

She frowns slightly. "But tomorrow's a workday."

"Yeah, but sometimes you gotta do what keeps you grounded. Music's my escape from reality. Keeps me sane."

I swear her eyes are shining now, "I want to see you play."

I raise an eyebrow. "Do you even know my style, sunshine? It might not be your cup of tea."

"I think I can handle it." She flashes a confident smirk.

"And what's that supposed to mean?"

Dodging my probing, she presses, "So, can I come or not?"

"Sure, why not. Rodrigo's planning to be there too," I say, watching her reaction closely, "You can join him."

Her face lights up. "Rodrigo's going? Then count me in. It's a date."

Before I can even get a word in, Maggie, ever the little scene-stealer, jumps into the conversation with her usual enthusiasm. "Guess what else Uncle Nick can do..."

I exhale slowly, trying to keep up with Maggie's revelations. "Anything else you'd like everyone to know about me, Maggs?"

She beams. "Uncle Nick travels a lot! And he's from the UK, like me, Mum, and Dad!"

Well, kiddo, that one was obvious.

I close my eyes briefly, and Ava's laughter rings out. "I had a hunch," she says, playfully nudging Maggie's chin.

Suddenly, Ava's watch buzzes. She checks it and jumps up. "Oh no, look at the time!"

Maggie looks up at her, all puppy dog eyes. "You're leaving?"

"I have to, honey," Ava says, slinging her bag over her shoulder and standing up.

Noticing Ava fumbling in her bag I say, "Don't worry about it, sunshine."

"I'm looking for my wallet," she insists, her search becoming more frantic.

"Forget it," I say again, a bit more firmly.

She finally looks up at me, "I can't let you pay for my lunch."

I shake my head, "Consider it a down payment. You can return the favor later."

Ava pauses, then nods, her expression softening. She leans down to Maggie, giving her a gentle kiss. "Lunch was fun. You be good, okay?"

Then, unexpectedly, Ava leans in and plants a soft kiss on my cheek. "Thanks, Nicholas. I'll make it up to you," she says softly before darting out of the restaurant.

I'm left standing here, slightly stunned.

Did she just call me Nicholas?

And did she just kiss me?

CHAPTER FIVE

AVA

As Petra heads off for her girls' night out with Deborah – Rodrigo's sister-in-law – I find myself walking alongside Rodrigo, heading to see Nick perform. It feels like a throwback to our old days.

"You good?" Rodrigo checks in as we step out of the burger joint into the chilly evening.

"Yep," I reply, wrapping my arms around myself against the brisk breeze. "Is the bar far?"

He glances at his watch. "Nope, just around the corner."

Curiosity gets the better of me. "Is this a regular thing for you? Watching Nick play?"

Rodrigo gives me a side glance and a half-smirk. "Not really. I mean, he's been playing there forever, but with all the back and forth between New York and Seattle, it's been a while."

"So, you've seen him play before?"

"Yeah, a few times. He's actually pretty good," Rodrigo admits.

"Does he play there often?"

"Pretty much every week, I think."

"Solo?" I ask.

He shakes his head. "No, with his band."

We stroll down the street, the bar lights now in sight.

"Would you have gone alone if I hadn't come along?"

Rodrigo chuckles, giving me a teasing look. "Curious, aren't you? If I didn't know better, I'd say you were interested in—"

I cut him off quickly, "Let's just go in."

As we step into the bar, it's like tumbling headfirst into a world that's strictly VIP. The lights are low, casting a soft, almost illicit glow over everything – like we're in a scene cut from a film noir.

The air's thick with smoke, twirling lazily from cigarettes. The buzz of conversations hums in the background, punctuated now and then by the clink of glasses – it's like this place has its own language. And there, smack in the middle of it all, is Nick. He's on stage, guitar in hand, looking every bit the center of this universe.

The moment we step deeper into the bar, it's as if Nick's got a sixth sense for our presence. His eyes flick up, locking onto us like a hawk spotting its prey. That guitar in his hands? It might as well be invisible now. He's all focused intensity, the kind that says you're the only thing in the room worth paying attention to. He saunters over, oozing the kind of confidence that's more street than school. He greets Rodrigo with a fist bump and then he turns to me. His look is a blend of wild and wicked, "Hey, sunshine," he drawls, "Didn't think you'd show."

"Well, I said I would," I shoot back, and he acknowledges it with a nod. Nick saunters to the bar, ordering a whiskey like it's his second language.

"What's your poison?" he throws over his shoulder at me, just as Rodrigo doubles up his own order.

"Uh, not really into drinking much," I admit, feeling a bit out of my element.

He lets out a low, knowing breath. "Figured this scene might not be your thing."

"I just wouldn't know what to pick."

He murmurs something to the bartender, then casually turns to Rodrigo. "Where's your other half tonight?"

"With Deborah. They needed some girl time," Rodrigo answers casually.

In that brief moment, the bartender's back with their drinks. Nick's handed something different, which he then extends to me. "Vodka with Coke," he says.

I take the cup, our fingers brushing. "Thanks."

The first chords ripple through the air, pulling Nick's attention away for a moment – showtime's calling. I take another sip of the drink he handed me, feeling its warmth spreading through me like liquid sin.

Man, this shit is good.

"You gonna play something special tonight?" Rodrigo asks.

Nick's eyes flick back to me. "Might have a song or two in mind."

He downs his whiskey as if it's just another part of the routine and strides towards the stage. But then, in a swift move, he pauses mid-step, turns back, and leans in close.

His breath is a whisper against my ear, "Stick around after the set." His fingers grazing mine as he pulls away.

Nick's words hang in the air as I watch him take the stage. There's an undeniable magnetism about him, a raw edge that makes it impossible to look away. *Or maybe I should stop drinking*.

Rodrigo nudges me, pulling me back to reality. "Looks like someone's caught your eye," he teases.

"Please, I'm just here for the music."

But who am I kidding?

Every note Nick plays feels like it's strung just for me. The way his fingers move over the strings, the intense focus in his eyes – *it's captivating*.

Rodrigo chuckles, sipping his drink. "You know, Nick's always had that effect on people. Draws them in like moths to a flame."

I take a deep breath, trying to steady my racing heart.

As the set rolls on, there's a part of me that's lost in the music, and another that's acutely aware of every glance Nick throws my way.

When the final song of the set ends, the crowd erupts into applause, and Nick's eyes find mine one last time before he disappears backstage. Rodrigo leans in, his voice low. "So, isn't he good?"

I nod, "He is."

He's more than good...

Rodrigo's eyes twinkle with mischief, "And it's not just the guitar skills that have you all starry-eyed, huh?"

I give my head a quick shake and make my way to the bar, silently setting down my cup.

—

NICK

Up on stage, with the guitar in my hands. This is where I'm supposed to lose myself in the chords, in the rhythm. But hell, all I can do is let my eyes keep sneaking peeks at Ava.

This is a bad idea. A really bad idea.

I shouldn't be fixating on her like this. Lucky for me, I'm the guy with the guitar, not the one crooning into the mic.

But there she is, in the crowd, impossible to miss. She's stunning, a real showstopper. And I had to go and tell her to 'stick around after the set' – *what was I thinking?*

I shake my head, trying to clear it.

Fuck this, I need a drink. I'm way too sober for this shit.

The final chord fades out, and we're off the stage. I head over to where Rod and Ava are, spotting Ava at the bar, grabbing another drink like the one I'd given her earlier.

"Man, that was epic. Even better than I remember," Rodrigo comments as Ava comes back, her drink in hand.

She's quiet, so I jump in. "So, sunshine, give me your verdict?"

She takes a sip, nodding slowly. "It was good."

Good? She's adorable, and it's driving me crazy.

Rodrigo excuses himself to grab more drinks. I lean in a bit closer to Ava, feigning a wounded ego. "Just 'good'? I was hoping for something like 'mind-blowing', 'life-changing', or 'earth-shattering'."

That gets a giggle out of her. "Okay, okay. It was definitely more than just good."

"Still a tough critic," I tease.

Rodrigo comes back with our drinks, but Ava hands me her cup, a playful warning in her eyes. "No funny business with this, okay? Just need a quick bathroom break." She heads off, leaving me here with a stupid grin on my face and her drink in my hand.

"Easy there, Thompson. I haven't seen you smile this much ever. Looks like 'sunshine' is melting your ice." Rodrigo breaks through my thoughts.

Damn it.

I try to play it cool, taking a casual sip from my drink while holding onto Ava's. "No clue what you're getting at, Gomez."

"Right," Rodrigo drawls, swirling the ice in his glass. "You know, for someone who asked me to come out, just so Ava could tag along, you're playing it pretty close to the chest."

I let out a slow breath, "I never explicitly said I wanted you to come so Ava could tag along."

Rodrigo raises an eyebrow. "Maybe not in so many words. But you kinda set me up, man. Made me the accidental wingman."

I cut in, a bit defensive, "Hold up, it wasn't a setup." I glance around, making sure Ava's not within earshot. "She said she wanted to come, so I might've hinted that you were likely showing up."

This is spiraling fast. Not how I planned it.

Rodrigo pushes further. "So, a lie by omission then?"

"If you want to call it a lie, it was a tiny one."

"Lies are lies, man, big or small."

Just as I'm about to argue back, Ava pops up, snagging her drink out of my hand and giving me a jolt. "Thanks for holding this, sir," she says with a smirk.

"I advise you to choose your next words very carefully" Rodrigo says loud enough only for me to hear.

"Is this where I find out about all your dark, twisted secrets, Nicholas Thompson?"

"What secrets? I'm an open book." I try to play it cool.

"More like a mystery novel," Rodrigo chimes in, clearly enjoying this a bit too much.

Ava takes a sip of her drink, her eyes never leaving mine. "So, this 'accidental wingman' thing... sounds intriguing."

Fuck my life. She caught more of that conversation than she was supposed to.

I can feel the heat rising to my face. "It's nothing. Just guys talking."

"Uh huh," she says.

Rodrigo has this devilish glint in his eye. "He's right. Just a little bro-to-bro chat, right, Nick?"

I shoot him a look that could kill, but Ava's already leaning in. "Bro-to-bro, huh? Must be some pretty deep stuff."

"Just the usual guy talk," I say, trying to deflect. "You know, sports, weather, the existential dread of our fleeting youth."

Ava laughs, the sound bright and easy. "Sounds intense. I hope you guys solved all the world's problems."

Rodrigo nudges me, "We're working on it. Nick here is full of surprises."

"I bet he is," Ava says.

"You have no idea," I murmur, unintentionally meeting her eyes.

Rodrigo clears his throat, obviously enjoying the show. "I'll leave you two to – whatever this is. I see a game of darts with my name on it."

As he wanders off, Ava turns to me, "So, got any other secrets you're hiding?"

I lean in closing the distance between us, a rush of adrenaline at our closeness. "Curious, aren't you?"

She steps in, matching my tone, her smile teasing. "Maybe just a bit."

This woman? She's clever as the devil and twice as pretty.

—

AVA

"So, how long have you been playing here?" I ask, trying to keep my voice steady despite the drinks.

The room's spinning just a bit – or maybe that's just Nick's unexpected smiles throwing me off balance. He doesn't usually dole them out so freely, right? Or is it the vodka playing tricks on me?

"Two years," he replies, his voice low and steady.

"Every night?"

"Just weekly," he says with a half-smirk.

"That's quite the commitment. Why stick around so long?"

He leans in, closing the gap between us, "Some nights, music's the only friend you've got."

His words hang in the air, and I take a moment to let them sink in. "Wow, didn't expect philosophy with my drink."

Nick shrugs, a shadow of a smile on his lips. "You're the one asking the deep questions."

"Well, aren't you just a beacon of darkness in this neon world?"

He raises an eyebrow, "Not all of us can be as bright as you, sunshine."

Before I can respond, Rodrigo cuts in. "Alright, party animals, time to head home. We've got the real world to face tomorrow."

I reluctantly grab my cardigan. "Yeah, reality calls."

Rodrigo gives Nick a casual wave. "See you around, man."

I hesitate, wanting to say something more, but words fail me. Instead, I offer a small, tentative wave, a smile tugging at the corners of my mouth. Nick nods, an unreadable expression in his eyes, before he turns and vanishes into the shadows of backstage.

Stepping out into the night, Rodrigo nudges me. "So, how'd you find the night?"

I let out a laugh. "Nick's a tough nut to crack."

Rodrigo grins. "Yeah, heart of gold, temper of a bull."

CHAPTER SIX

AVA

Two weeks post-Jax's New York exodus, and I've successfully ghosted every attempt he's made to reconnect. It's not that I don't care – it's just that every buzz of my phone, every 'Jax' lit up on my screen, feels like a flashback to a romantic movie I'm no longer cast in.

Work's been my trusty old distraction – that, and the absence of Maggie. Odd, how missing a kid was once a relief, but with Maggie, it's like missing a piece of sunshine.

Rodrigo's sudden voice startles me, and I nearly jump out of my skin. "Geez, Rodrigo! You nearly gave me a heart attack!" I playfully shove his arm.

He's all smirks, "Caught you daydreaming, didn't I?"

I slump back in my chair, rolling my eyes. "What now?"

Rodrigo leans against my desk, all casual. "Fancy a little mission? Need you to play delivery girl to Nick's office."

I raise an eyebrow. "Seriously? Why can't Nick swing by himself? Or, I don't know, wait until tomorrow?"

He shrugs, that annoyingly charming grin not leaving his face. "Because I'm asking you, Ava. Got a problem helping out your boss?"

I cross my arms. "Sounds more like you're helping out Nick, not me. What's in it for me, huh?"

He leans in, a glint in his eyes. "Between you and me, I think Nick might just need an excuse to see you."

My heart skips a beat, and I can feel my face heat up. "Excuse to see me? Rodrigo, don't start with your matchmaking games."

He throws his hands up in mock surrender. "I'm just messing with you. Nick really needs these documents, and you're the only one I trust to get them there safely."

I sigh, taking the documents from him. "Alright, fine. But this isn't going to become a regular thing."

Rodrigo winks. "You're the best, Ava. And hey, who knows? Maybe you'll enjoy the little detour."

I shake my head and head out of the office.

It's just a quick drop-off. Nothing else.

Why did Rodrigo's joke affect me so much?

What if he really wanted an excuse to see me? Do I actually want it to be true?

No way, Ava. You're just overthinking things.

Let's face it, Nicholas Thompson is an enigma wrapped in a riddle, with a hint of charm lurking beneath his tough-guy facade. *But that's all it is — a hint.*

First off, it's laughable to think Nick would actually need an excuse to see me. The guy barely acknowledges my existence, flashing a rare smile my way maybe twice. Our interactions have been a mix of him either blatantly ignoring me or throwing me off with his brooding intensity.

And second, I'm probably just reading too much into Rodrigo's joke. My emotions are all over the place lately, with everything that's gone down with Jax. Rodrigo's tease was just that — a tease.

—

I'm flipping through some legal documents, completely absorbed in my work, when a knock on the door breaks my focus.

"Yeah?" I call out, not looking up from the papers.

Hannah peeks in. "Nick, you've got a visitor. A woman."

"A woman?" I echo, "Who is it?"

"It's Ms. Ava Adams."

Ava? Here? This is something I wasn't expecting. I thought I was finally getting her out of my head, with Ella back and Maggie no longer dragging me into visits. I've been struggling to shake her image from my mind, her laugh echoing in my dreams, and now, she's right here at my office. *Talk about bad timing*.

"Let her in, Hannah," I say, attempting to sound indifferent, but my pulse quickens in anticipation.

The door swings open and there she is, Ava Adams, looking even more stunning than I remember. She's in a pale pink dress, her blonde hair flowing in waves that seem to capture the light. I quickly school my features into a mask of indifference.

"What brings you here, Ava?"

She steps forward, holding out a black document folder. "Rodrigo sent me with these papers," she says, her voice as smooth.

Standing up, I smooth out my shirt, trying to appear composed as I walk around the desk to where Ava stands. I reach out for the documents, and she hands them over. Opening the folder, I expect to find something related to my current case, but instead, I'm met with Intellectual Property papers, clearly not related to my work. *What's going on here?*

"I have no clue what these are about," I admit, flipping through them.

I hear Ava's sharp intake of breath as she tries to make sense of Rodrigo's request. "Rodrigo said they were important, and I needed to bring them straight to you today. Maybe your client thought you worked together and gave them to Rodrigo instead?" she suggests.

Flipping through the pages, I find a note attached, scribbled in Rodrigo's handwriting. "One day, you'll thank me for this. Ask her out. Rod."

Bloody hell, Rodrigo...

—

AVA

As I'm about to leave Nick's office, he suddenly calls out, "Ava." Hearing him say my name sends an unexpected flutter through my chest.

"Yeah?" I turn back, finding him buried in the documents, his expression unreadable.

"You know, at lunch the other day with Maggie, you dashed off, and I covered your meal. So technically, you owe me one."

Reaching for my wallet, I'm ready to settle the debt, but he stops me with a shake of his head. "I'm not after your money, sunshine. I meant you owe me a favor."

"What do you mean?"

He finally looks up, "Remember mentioning those leather pants of yours?"

A reluctant smile tugs at my lips. "Yeah, I remember mentioning my black leather trousers."

"Well," he continues, closing the folder and setting it aside, "Maggie's with her mum this weekend, but I'll be taking her for a motorbike ride. You should join us."

The idea gives me pause. Nick and me on a motorbike? That's a scene I would never picture.

He reads my hesitation and leans in. "It's not a request, Ms. Adams. Tell me where to pick you up."

I counter, half-joking, "A motorbike ride with a kid and me? Doesn't sound too safe."

He grins, "No excuses today, Ava. It's a yes or a yes."

"Alright, how about I meet you both somewhere?"

"Perfect," he nods. "And don't forget those leather pants. It's an unwritten rule of the road."

I'm almost out the door when a thought strikes me. Turning back, I call out, "Nick?"

He hums a response.

"How am I supposed to get in touch with you?"

He smirks, a rare sight that sends a shock through me. "I'll find a way to let you know, Ava. Don't worry about it."

"But you don't have my number," I point out.

"Trust me, I'll manage," he says.

—

NICK

"Rod, are you actually serious right now?" I ask, incredulous, as soon as he picks up the phone.

Rodrigo bursts into laughter. "Nick, you've got to admit, it was a brilliant idea. You'll thank me later."

I let out a heavy sigh, "This is madness, mate..."

There's a pause before he asks, "So, did you ask her out?"

I grumble, "Do you realize how risky that was? I was completely blindsided when she walked into my office. A little heads-up would've been nice."

Rodrigo's tone is matter-of-fact. "If I had warned you, you wouldn't have played along."

"And you think your plan actually worked?"

Rodrigo's voice turns anxious. "Nick, please don't tell me you messed this chance up."

"Rod, what 'chance' are you talking about? Since when do you play matchmaker for me?"

"I've known you for years, Nick. I can tell when you're into someone."

I scoff. "Rodrigo, you know me well enough to know I don't do this little thing called 'love'."

He's almost pleading now. "For fuck's sake. Just tell me you asked her out, Nicholas."

"What if I did? You might be putting Ms. Sunshine under the bus, or in this case, under me!"

"That's a bit risqué, Nick," he jokes.

I shake my head in disbelief.

"I trust you won't hurt her," he says.

"That's assuming a lot," I shoot back.

Rodrigo's voice softens. "Nick, she's different from the others. You and me both know it."

I sigh heavily. "Yes, she's a ray of sunshine, Rod. And you've complicated things."

He's persistent. "So, you did ask her out?"

I try to shift the blame back to him. "Why, Rodrigo? Why did you have to meddle?"

"She needs to meet new people, and you need a break from work."

"I didn't ask for a social secretary. And why does she need new people in her life?"

Rodrigo hesitates before spilling the beans. "She just ended a long-term relationship."

I stop pacing, that hits a nerve. "Brilliant. So, I'm what, a rebound? I'm not cut out for this."

He tries to interject, but I'm not having it.

"I'm not Mr. Sunshine, Rod. I can't fix her heartbreak. You shouldn't have done this."

He cuts in. "But Thompson, did you ask her out?"

I let out a frustrated sigh. "Yes, Gomez. I did ask her out."

—

AVA

As I step out of the car, the tranquility of the place hits me. The air is crisp and fresh, and birds chirp in the background, painting a picture perfect for a day out. I make my way down a path, following Nick's instructions to a quaint clearing.

I find Nick and Maggie at a picnic table, surrounded by a spread of picnic goodies. Maggie's face lights up as she sees me. "Ava!" she exclaims, rushing over for a hug. "I missed you so much!"

I return her hug, "This place is gorgeous, Maggie. I had no idea we were having a picnic."

Maggie beams, proud. "Uncle Nick and I love picnics!"

Catching Nick's eye, I notice he's dressed down today in black leather trousers and a casual t-shirt, a stark contrast to his usual polished look.

He stands up, looking slightly uncomfortable in his casual getup, and grunts, "We've got to eat."

I suppress a chuckle, eyeing his leather trousers.

Before I can comment, he warns, "Don't start with me about the pants. Motorbike rules."

"I wouldn't dare," I reply.

He raises an eyebrow, "Sure you wouldn't."

Maggie's excitement cuts through the air. "Uncle Nick! Show Ava your bike!"

Nick leads me over to his black motorbike. "Wow, what a beautiful motorcycle," I remark, glancing at Maggie.

"It's a motorbike, Ava," Maggie corrects me with a cute smile.

Nick laughs, looking down at his niece. "It's both, Maggs. Ava says 'motorcycle' because that's what they call it in the States."

Maggie looks puzzled but then shrugs.

"But Ava also says 'trousers' instead of 'pants'," Nick teases, "Americans just don't know how to say the words correctly." He winks at Maggie, and she bursts into giggles.

"They do, Uncle Nick!" she protests, still giggling.

Jumping in, I say, "Speaking of pants, I brought my black leather pants as requested." I flash a smile at Nick, imitating his accent playfully.

Nick gives me a quick, appreciative once-over and meets my gaze. "Yes, you did, sunshine. Definitely did." His voice has a strange hint of warmth.

Maggie, seizing the moment, tugs at my hand. "Uncle Nick, can Ava ride with us before we eat?"

Nick gives me a questioning look. "Have you ever ridden a motorbike before?"

I shake my head, "No, never."

Nick nods. "Alright, Maggs. First, I need to teach Ava how to be safe on a motorbike."

Maggie nods vigorously, pushing me gently towards Nick. "You're going to love it, Ava!"

Nick climbs onto his bike and gestures for Maggie to sit nearby. She dashes to a tree and settles down to watch us.

As I stand next to Nick, I sense him giving me another quick look.

Is that a smirk on his face?

Nicholas Thompson, you're full of surprises.

"Hop on," he says. As I hesitate, Nick gives me a side-glance. "Just swing a leg over, like a bicycle. But you'll be right behind me this time."

Awkwardly, I maneuver myself onto the bike, trying my best not to make contact with him. But it's a tight fit. "Okay, I think I've got it," I say, more to myself than to Nick.

Suddenly, Nick reaches back, his warm fingers finding mine in an unexpected move. He guides my hands around his waist, and it's like electricity surges through me. The first real touch, and it's as if a current passes between us, setting my skin ablaze.

Fuck, fuck, fuck!

I don't like this.

I shouldn't.

I start to pull away, my heart thudding against my ribcage. But Nick's not having any of it. He revs the engine, and I'm thrown forward. Instinct takes over, and I wrap my arms around him, holding on for dear life.

"Safety first," his voice is a low rumble.

Maggie's innocent laughter echoes in the background, but it's drowned out by the pounding of my heart and the rush of blood in my ears. My heart is beating faster than I thought it ever could.

Pulled close against him, I can smell his cologne, mixed with a hint of leather and something inherently Nick. It's intoxicating, and my cheeks flush.

"You need to hug Uncle Nick, Ava!" Maggie shouts.

Nick turns his head slightly, his eyes meeting mine, "She's right, you should hug Uncle Nick. It's for your own safety," he says, his voice low.

The engine roars beneath us, and I instinctively hold on tighter. "Wait! What about helmets? And Maggie?" I call out, my voice tinged with panic.

Nick breaks into laughter, the vibrations running through his body. "I was just messing with you. We're not going anywhere without Maggie—" His laughter is contagious. "—and there's no need to try and cut off my oxygen, sunshine." he adds.

I loosen my grip and try to regain my composure, "Sorry, got a bit carried away there."

Maggie's still bubbling with excitement, her laughter echoing around us. I watch as Nick dismounts, his movements smooth. He ruffles Maggie's hair affectionately. "Okay, Maggs, let's dig into that picnic. Afterward, we'll talk motorbikes."

—

NICK

"Next time, let me know if we're picnicking," Ava says. "I would've whipped up something."

She said 'next time'.

I gesture towards the spread on the table where Maggie is demolishing a slice of pizza. "We're good on food, trust me. Plus," I add with a smirk, "It's a surprise picnic. No prior notice allowed, right, Maggs?" I give Maggie a wink.

"That's really sweet, Maggie," Ava says, her smile lighting up her face. Maggie just nods, focused on her pizza and iced tea.

I steal glances at Ava, noticing how those leather pants of hers are doing things to me. She's all innocent charm up top, but those pants scream pure sin — it's like she's walking that fine line between angel and devil, and it's throwing me off balance.

The way she moves, completely oblivious to the captivating show she's putting on, is enough to drive a man wild. She's like a walking, talking contradiction — a delicate rose with thorns that promise both pleasure and pain.

"Ava, do you have a boyfriend?" Maggie's words hit like a cold shower, snapping me back to reality and cutting my thoughts clean in half.

"Margrett," I scold, giving her a warning look. "Ease up with the interrogation, will you?"

"It's okay," Ava says quickly, tucking a strand of hair behind her ear, a hint of pink on her cheeks. "No, I don't have a boyfriend, Maggie."

"But you're so pretty!" Maggie's mouth hangs open in disbelief.

Ava's giggle is soft and genuine, "Thank you, sweetie."

But Maggie's not done. She turns her big eyes on me. "Don't you think Ava's pretty, Uncle Nick?"

Trying to maintain my cool, I meet Ava's gaze briefly. "She's not bad to look at," I say casually. Ava's eyes dart away, but not before I catch a deeper blush on her cheeks.

Maggie, being Maggie, pushes further. "You and Ava should be boyfriend and girlfriend!"

Ava opens her mouth to respond, but I cut in before she can get a word out. "Maggie, we talked about appropriate topics, remember?"

"But you don't have a girlfriend either," she counters, as if it's the most logical solution in the world.

"That's because I'm difficult to love," I say.

Maggie giggles, reaching for her drink, but the way Ava's avoiding my gaze tells me she's thinking about Maggie's words.

What have you gotten us into, Margrett?

"You're not difficult to love, Nick," Ava says, her voice soft but firm, her beautiful blue eyes locked on mine now. "Maybe you've just been asking the wrong people."

I'm momentarily floored, and for a split second, I'm speechless, which doesn't happen often.

Ava seems to realize she's ventured into uncharted territory and backpedals with an apology, sitting up straighter. "I'm sorry, I shouldn't have said that. It's not my place."

"You're quite wrong, sunshine. The Devil and I are thick as thieves. And let's face it, who in their right mind would love the Devil?" I tease.

But Ava doesn't back down. "Maybe that's what draws people to you." She's not flinching, and it's both unnerving and exhilarating.

Just as the tension between us thickens, Maggie, oblivious to the undercurrents, pipes up, "Can we go for a ride on your bike now, Uncle Nick?"

Ava looks away, her usual spark dimming a bit. "I'll just watch. I'm not too sure about riding a motorcycle. Maybe leather trousers aren't really my thing."

"I'd say you fit the part quite well in those pants." The moment the words escape my lips, I mentally kick myself.

Bloody hell, Nick. Too forward.

Ava's cheeks flush a deeper shade of pink, and I'm left wondering what the hell I'm doing.

Ava Adams, what are you doing to me?

"Alright, Maggs, time for that ride," I say, trying to shake off the awkward moment as I adjust Maggie's helmet. "Last chance, Ava. Join us?"

Ava laughs, shaking her head. "I highly doubt your bike is equipped for a party of three."

"Oh, so now you're doubting my expertise?" I tease.

Ava tilts her head, "Is it safe, though?"

"Absolutely. You in the back, Maggs up front. Just hold on tight," I assure her, even though my heart's doing weird flips.

"And what about helmets?" Ava asks, her hands on her hips in a way that's distractingly appealing.

"Use mine," I offer, trying to maintain my composure.

She immediately shakes her head. "No, you should have it. Safety first, right?"

I shrug. "It's just around the block. We'll be fine."

"That's not very reassuring," she retorts, her eyebrows knitting together in concern.

"Don't worry, I've done this plenty of times."

"That's not something to be proud of," she counters.

"I'm not proud," I clarify, "Just experienced. What's the harm?"

Ava's eyes narrow slightly. "Still a no."

"Why so concerned?"

"I don't want anything to happen to you," she admits, her voice softer than before.

As I'm trying to register what she just said, Maggie looks up at us, her eyes wide. "Is Uncle Nick gonna die?"

"No," Ava and I say in unison.

"I'm not going anywhere," I assure them both, my eyes lingering on Ava. "Come on, just get on."

With a hesitant breath, Ava gives in and climbs onto the bike behind me. I hand her my helmet, and she struggles a bit with it. Chuckling, I hop off to help her, then jump back on. "Hold on tight," I remind her.

For a moment, Ava hesitates.

"Need another adrenaline rush?" I tease her. Then she wraps her arms around me, and I can feel her warmth against my back, her presence sending an unexpected thrill through me.

The bike roars to life under us, Ava's grip tightening, making me feel a dangerous sense of rightness.

Ava Adams, you might just be my kind of danger.

CHAPTER SEVEN

Nick's motorcycle ride strikes the perfect balance between thrilling and safe, especially with Maggie and me onboard.

When we finally pull over, Maggie's bubbling with energy. "More, more, more! Uncle Nick!" she chants, her enthusiasm infectious.

Nick', with all the patience in the world, helps Maggie off the bike. "That's enough for now," he says, then catches me fumbling with my helmet. "Need some help with that?"

I nod, grateful for the rescue. Nick steps in close, his hands deftly removing my helmet, and there's this fleeting moment where his fingers graze my hair. "Thanks," I say, trying to hide the flutter in my stomach.

"No problem," he replies, and I swear there's a hint of a smile on his face.

Out of the blue, Maggie lets out a scream, and we both whirl around, hearts pounding. Relief floods through me when we see her laughing, a big, friendly German Shepherd playfully licking her face.

Nick runs a hand through his hair, a combination of exasperation and relief. "Maggie, you're going to give me a heart attack one of these days."

I chuckle, trying to calm my racing heart. "You and me both."

Maggie's completely enamored with the dog now. "Uncle Nick, can I play with him a bit?" she asks, her eyes sparkling with delight.

Nick nods toward the dog's owner, "That depends on the owner's permission, Maggie."

The owner, a man holding the leash, nods with a smile. "Sure, no problem. We're just having a picnic over there," he gestures. "Dante loves kids."

Maggie's already off, her laughter filling the air as she runs around with the dog. "Thanks," Nick calls out to the man, "Just so you know, she's got enough energy to run a marathon."

The man laughs. "Dante can keep up. We're just there if you need us," he says, pointing to where his wife is waving at us.

Nick watches them for a moment, then turns back to me, shaking his head. "That girl's going to tire out the dog before lunch."

We settle back at the picnic table, and I ask, "So, you and Maggie... you've always been this close?"

He looks over at her, playing happily, then back at me. "Not always. Life's complicated."

I nod, "But she's only four."

"And?" Nick's eyes meet mine.

"Nothing," I say quickly, not wanting to pry too deep. "Just curious."

Nick's expression softens a bit. "Maggie's special, that's all. She makes it easy to be close." He glances at her again, and I can see the affection in his eyes. "Let's just say, she's good at breaking down walls."

"She's just a little kid. Bright, sure, but still so young," I point out, watching Maggie play.

Nick's eyes finally meet mine, "What's your angle, Ava?"

I falter under his gaze. "I... It's just... When did you become so involved in her life?" I manage, trying to keep my voice steady.

His expression shifts. "When my brother died. Maggie was just two, and I had to step in, play the role of the parent she needed. It wasn't in my plan, but life's funny like that.

"Can I ask about your brother?" I venture, though a part of me screams to back off.

Nick looks at me, his gaze sharp. "I don't talk about him," he says simply, ending that line of questioning.

"I'm sorry, I didn't mean to pry."

He shrugs it off. "No worries."

I hesitate, then add, "I was just curious. About you."

"Curiosity can be dangerous, Ava."

"I just wanted to understand you better."

Nick's response is calm. "There's not much to understand."

"I think there's more to you than you let on."

He turns to me, one eyebrow arched. "Enlighten me, then."

I take the plunge. "You're a closed book, Nick. Hard to read."

"Then you'd better ask the right questions."

I take a deep breath. "You're not easy to get along with, are you?"

His gaze intensifies. "Yet here you are, trying. Why's that, Ava?"

I'm at a loss, my heart racing. "Remember, you invited me here."

He nods, acknowledging. "True, Ms. Adams."

"So, why am I here, Nick?"

His answer surprises me. "I suppose I needed a ray of sunshine to brighten my dark world. And you, Ava, are that ray of sunshine my soul needed."

His words leave me speechless, my cheeks burning. He stands up, leaving me there to ponder his unexpected confession, and walks over to Maggie, who's still playing with the dog.

Nick's words echo in my mind, a ray of sunshine in his dark world. *What is that supposed to mean?*

—

NICK

What in the bloody hell was I thinking, telling Ava she's the sunshine my soul needed? I must be losing it. She's just getting over a relationship, and here I am, spewing poetic lines like some lovestruck Romeo.

Rodrigo's definitely getting a piece of my mind later.

I steal another glance at Ava, still sitting there, looking stunned. I feel this magnetic pull towards her, *but it's complete madness*. Ava's like a walking ray of sunshine, and me? I'm more of a brooding storm cloud. She deserves someone who can match her radiance, not a guy who's more likely to bring a downpour.

As I approach Maggie, her infectious laughter with Dante is a stark contrast to the chaos in my head. I force a smile, trying to immerse myself in her simple joy and push away the complex emotions Ava's stirred in me.

"Uncle Nick, Dante's fun!" Maggie's bright voice snaps me back to reality.

"Yeah, he's a real comedian," I reply, trying to sound upbeat. But even as I watch Maggie play, my mind keeps wandering back to Ava. It's like she's cracked open a door I've kept shut for years, and now, all these unwelcome feelings are flooding in.

I shake my head, attempting to dispel the thoughts. Ava needs someone who can shine alongside her, not someone who's constantly wrestling with shadows.

My gloomy soul doesn't deserve her sunshine.

Maggie's excitement is like a live wire, sparking the air as she shouts, "Uncle Nick, come play with Dante and me!"

I kneel down to Dante's level, giving him a friendly pat. "Not sure if Dante's really up for playing with me."

Just then, Maggie turns her attention to Ava. "Ava!" she calls, waving her over with a catching excitement. "Come play with us!"

Ava's laughter echoes as she approaches. She kneels down beside us, her hand brushing my shoulder. "Ever had a dog, Nick?" she asks, her voice soft, and her smile gentle.

I play it casual, avoiding direct eye contact. "Yeah, had a couple of Belgian Shepherds. Always had a thing for these guys."

Ava seems puzzled as she looks at Dante. "I thought he was a German Shepherd."

With a chuckle, I correct her, "Nope, Dante here is a Belgian." I focus on rubbing Dante's belly, which he seems to thoroughly enjoy.

"So, a dog person, then?" Ava asks crouching next to me, her presence impossible to ignore.

"Yeah, you could say that," I try my best to keep my attention on the dog.

Ava's smile doesn't waver. "I lean more towards cats," she admits with a light giggle.

"Well, that figures. Cats are like women, dogs are like men – more loyal," I tease, watching her reaction.

Ava gives my arm a playful tap, her gaze fixed on Dante. "I'm not too sure about that," she counters playfully. In a moment of unguarded spontaneity, I find my hand touching hers, only to quickly withdraw it, refocusing on the dog.

Maggie, ever the inquisitive one, jumps in with a curious question. "You and Uncle Nick couldn't live together then?"

Before I can even form a response, Ava beats me to it. "Of course, we could! Nick would just have to get used to a cat around."

"And Ava would need to get used to a dog," I add, trying to keep the conversation light for Maggie's sake.

As she speaks, her smile is as bright as ever. "Actually, that's where you're wrong, Nick. Cat people aren't as single-minded as you dog lovers. We appreciate all kinds of animals."

"Wow, Ava. Here I was, thinking you were all sweetness and rainbows. Clearly, I underestimated you."

Maggie jumps back into the conversation. "So, does that mean you'll live together?"

I pause for a moment, throwing the ball back in Ava's court. "What do you say, sunshine? Should we start house hunting?"

Ava meets my challenge head-on, turning to Maggie with a playful glint in her eye. "Well, Maggie, as tempting as that sounds, I think living with your uncle might be a bit too much of an adventure for me."

"Fair enough," I concede, standing up.

—

AVA

Collapsed on my couch, shoes flung off, I'm wrestling with my own thoughts.

"What's up with you, Ava?" I ask myself out loud. Today's been a whirlwind with Nick and Maggie, lighting a spark in me I didn't even know existed.

"Is it just his mystery thing?" I wonder, feeling my pulse race. There's something about Nick, how he's all closed up but then there's these moments, rare and shiny, where he cracks a smile or laughs, and it feels like winning the lottery.

With Jax, everything was comfy, like an old, cozy blanket. But this thing with Nick? It's like a wild ride, scary and exciting at the same time, miles away from the safe zone Jax and I had.

I close my eyes, taking a deep breath. Nick, with his moody vibe, and Maggie, all happiness and giggles, have stirred up something fierce in me.

This feels like a firecracker in my chest.

"What're you doing, girl?" I mutter to myself.

—

NICK

I stride into Rodrigo's place, with Maggie tagging along like my personal shadow. "Listen up," I announce, coming to a dramatic halt and pivoting to face him, "I need you to understand one thing, my friend. I am never, ever doing this again. Seriously, not a snowball's chance in hell."

Maggie's attention immediately shifts to Rodrigo's Golden Retriever, and she cheers, "Puppy!"

Rodrigo, looking utterly perplexed, shuts the door behind us. "What's going on here?"

"Ava, Rodrigo! Ava is what's going on!" I exclaim, the frustration bubbling up. "Your brilliant plan to label me as Ava's 'band-aid' has gone sideways faster than a raccoon in a garbage can." I realize I might have cranked up the volume a tad too much and wince.

Petra emerges from the kitchen, curiosity in her eyes. "What's happening with Ava?"

Rodrigo flashes a sly grin, fixing his gaze on me, running his hand through his hair in that infuriatingly charming way of his. "Nothing to fret about, Bird. Nick's just being Nick."

I inhale deeply and give Rodrigo a begrudging nod. "Sure, whatever."

Rodrigo leans in closer, "Would you mind keeping an eye on Maggie for a bit, Petra?" He clearly wants to have a private chat, and Petra takes the hint, nodding and fading into the background.

I narrow my eyes at Rodrigo and growl, "I swear, I could strangle you right now."

"So, what's the deal?" He grins.

"The deal? Rod, I'm as lost as a penguin in the Sahara," I grumble.

Rodrigo chuckles, leaning against the wall. "And how's that my fault, Nick?"

"You're the one who unleashed her on me! If she hadn't walked into my office, I wouldn't have asked her out, and I wouldn't be standing here, contemplating the meaning of life!"

"But what's happening, exactly?" Rodrigo pushes for answers.

"I don't even know," I sigh, tossing my head back in exasperation. "She's like a damn lighthouse, mate. And I'm just a lost ship in the dark sea."

"It's clearly your kind of lighthouse. I sent her your way because I knew you needed a guiding star," Rodrigo counters.

"No, I didn't. I was perfectly fine before all this," I argue.

"Come on, Nick," Rodrigo tilts his head, wearing that annoying 'I know better' expression. "You look at her like she's the missing piece to your puzzle."

"Don't you dare start with that 'love' talk," I warn Rodrigo, pointing a finger at him. "You haven't seen us together long enough to draw conclusions."

Rodrigo throws his hands up in surrender. "I'm just calling it like I see it."

I take a deep breath, attempting to cool my frustration. "I need some clarity here," I start. "She's your friend, right?"

"She's practically family to me," Rodrigo replies.

"Why on earth would you want her tangled up with someone like me? You know my track record."

"That's precisely why—" Rodrigo begins, but I cut him off.

"—And you told me she was in a long-term relationship!"

"With one of my best mates," Rodrigo admits.

"What the hell, Rod," I mutter, running a hand through my hair. "What are you getting me into?"

"Nick, Jax is like a brother to me too, and if I'm doing this, it's because I genuinely believe you're a better fit for her than he is," Rodrigo states seriously, which only makes me grumble.

"This is insane," I turn away from Rodrigo and pace in his hallway.

"They were in a long-term relationship, and Ava sort of lost herself in it," Rodrigo explains.

I stop and stare at him, curiosity piqued. "Lost herself? What do you mean?"

"They were friends in New York before they started dating. We all worked together. Jax left New York, and Ava stayed, but she never really connected with anyone else. She threw herself into work and never even considered dating," Rodrigo elaborates. "But then Jax returned to New York when Ava was already in Seattle with me, and he had a car accident. Ava rushed back to be with him, and they rekindled their relationship. Jax ended up moving to Seattle and stayed here for about a year."

"I'm not sure you should be sharing all this with me," I protest. "Feels too personal, Rod."

"Listen, I need you to understand why I think you're the better choice for Ava compared to Jax," Rodrigo insists. "Ava changed after she got back together with Jax. She was still a shining star, but her light dimmed a bit. For a whole year, Ava wasn't herself. That relationship started holding her back. They were great until they weren't. Then, she found out Jax did something I can't condone, and she ended things."

"Let me guess, she started shining again after that?" I interject.

"Not quite," Rodrigo corrects me. "She was miserable for a while, and then you walked into the picture. After your first encounter in my office, something shifted in her. The Ava I knew and loved came back to life after talking to you."

"We barely even talked. I mean, I was a total jerk the first time we crossed paths," I point out.

"And still, you managed to make a difference in her life and help her find herself again," Rodrigo states, a knowing smile on his face.

"Rod, I get what you're saying, but—" I start, but Rodrigo doesn't let me finish.

"I know the truth, Nick. I know Ava, and I know you," he asserts.

"But, Rod, it feels rushed. She needs time to heal, not me suddenly popping up in her life like this."

"You're already there, Nick." Rodrigo reminds me.

"I don't want to intrude into her life like this, I don't want to be the cause of her pain," I explain.

"See? You're already thinking about her feelings. When was the last time you did that, Nick? When have you ever been concerned about someone else?" Rodrigo challenges, leaving me without a response.

CHAPTER EIGHT

AVA

My phone buzzes and I casually unlock it, getting comfortable on the couch.

The message catches my eye, "Can I come over?" it reads. And then, the bombshell: "It's Nick."

I practically leap from my seat, my heart doing a little race at the sight of his name. I remain frozen for a beat, then another text rolls in, "I know where you live." I can't help but laugh – it's like a scene right out of 'You.'

"Stalker much?"

"Blame Rodrigo," Nick replies.

"Is everything okay with Maggie?" I quickly ask.

"Yes, found something and thought you'd be the best to handle it. I have no clue what to do," he types back.

I'm growing impatient with text messages, not really understanding what's going on, so I decide to dial his number. The moment he answers, I cut to the chase, "What's wrong?"

"Steady, sunshine. Couldn't resist hearing my voice a moment longer?" his voice a deep sound.

"It's just simpler this way," I say, twirling a strand of hair as I lounge on the couch. "We were getting nowhere"

Nick continues, "There's something I've got here with me, and I don't know what to do with it."

"And why on earth would I have the answer?"

Suddenly, my phone starts buzzing, and oh boy, it's a FaceTime call from him.

I find myself in a hair-fixing dilemma, my fingers attempting to tame my unruly locks. But before I can make much progress, he chimes in, "Ava, don't waste your time on your hair, pretty sure you look stunning. I'm FaceTiming you, so trust me, it's a life-or-death situation."

I give in and accept the call, revealing him seated in his car. "Well," he starts, raising a tiny, furry bundle in front of the camera, "What am I supposed to do with this?"

"Oh, dear Lord, Nick!" I exclaim, covering my mouth with my hand while holding the phone with the other. "Where did you find that?" I ask, eyeing the little grey kitten with sparkling amber eyes he's cradling.

"I was walking from the office to my car when I heard something," he explains as the kitten lets out another meow. "I went to investigate, and there it was, this tiny guy."

"Now what?"

"That's how this all began, remember?" he reminds me. "You're the cat person here, not me. I need your help dealing with this tiny troublemaker."

"Bring it over!" I demand, excitement running through me.

"Sure thing, just text me your address," he gently places the kitten down.

"Hold on a second, you said you knew where I live."

"It seemed like the most amusing way to kick off a conversation with you," he confesses, earning a laugh from me.

"You know, 'Hey, this is Nick,' would have worked too," I tease.

"Nah, that's too ordinary," he says with a hint of a smirk.

"Alright then, I'll send it to you."

"Fantastic. See you soon, love," he says before ending the call.

Shit, shit, shit. How did this turn into Nick coming over to my place?

—

NICK

I park my car in front of Ava's building, cradling the kitten in my arms, and head towards the entrance. I send her a quick message to let her know I've arrived.

In the lobby, I locate the elevator and take it up to the fifth floor, anticipation building with each floor passing by.

As I walk down the hallway, Ava comes into view. She's standing at her apartment door with it wide open, her hands flying to her mouth in delight when she spots the kitten.

Does she always look this stunning? Even with her hair in a messy bun, no makeup, and dressed in light blue pajama shorts and a tank top – she's an absolute vision to behold.

"Oh my, look at how adorable!" she exclaims as I approach.

"Well, I do try my best. Thank you for the compliment," I tease, earning a warm smile from her.

"Not you, Nicholas. The cat," she says, gently taking the kitten from my arms. "Come in."

"Ms. Adams, would you kindly refrain from addressing me so formally? For a moment there, I felt like I was talking to my mother."

Inside Ava's apartment, I close the door behind me, and she asks, "Is it a boy or a girl?"

I raise my hands sheepishly and admit, "I must confess, I checked. I won't pretend I didn't, but at least I can tell you it's a male."

Ava's laughter is a beautiful sound. "You're such a sweetheart, aren't you?" she coos to the kitten in a baby voice. *She's utterly charming.*

"What do you have in mind for the kitty?"

"I'm not entirely sure yet, but we can't let him roam the streets, can we?" she responds while cradling the kitten in her arms.

"So, you'll be taking care of him, then?"

"I suppose I will, but I'm not prepared for it. I don't have litter, food, or toys. My apartment isn't even cat-friendly," she says.

"Don't worry, we can handle that. Some stores might still be open, and we can grab the essentials," I suggest, glancing at my wristwatch before locking eyes with her.

"We?" Ava's eyes light up. "Are you coming with me?"

"I was the one who brought you this little guy, wasn't I? It's the least I can do."

"Nick, you're a lifesaver!" Ava exclaims as she hands me the kitten. She then jumps and claps with excitement, rising up on her tiptoes to give me a tender peck on the cheek. "I'm just going to get changed quickly. Thanks again," she says with a smile before darting off into the hallway.

—

Ava has already set up the litter box for the kitten and arranged food and water on the black and white tiled floor of the kitchen.

As I lounge on the couch with the furry feline on my lap, "Have you decided on a name for this little troublemaker yet?" I turn to catch Ava's eye.

"Not yet," she replies while tenderly stroking the cat's belly.

I chuckle and suggest, "Well, how about 'Nick'?"

Ava grins, "Oh, really?"

"Absolutely, just look at those amber eyes, much like mine and perhaps even more intense. This way, you'll never forget about me." I tease her.

"How could anyone ever forget about you, Nicholas? You are not exactly forgettable," she says, arching an eyebrow at me.

"Firstly, we are back to using given names, aren't we? Secondly, what do you mean by that?"

"I mean, you have a personality that is quite distinctive and one-of-a-kind," she smiles.

"I'm not quite sure if you're having a go at me or not, Ava."

She lets out a soft giggle and says, "You are quite the mystery, Nick. You have a tendency to keep things to yourself, and that just makes me more intrigued by you. It's as if you've got me thinking about you even when you're not here."

I take advantage of the moment, cutting in as she tries to rectify her words, "Well, well, sunshine. It seems that I've left quite an impact on you if you're pondering over me in my absence."

"That's not what I meant to say," she says, her cheeks flushing pink.

"There's no need to deny it," I continue to tease her.

She hesitates for a moment before cautiously asking, "May I ask why?"

"Why what?"

"Why are you so guarded around me," her blue eyes meet mine before breaking contact.

"I'm not quite sure I understand."

"All I know about you is what Maggie told me and wasn't even supposed to," her attention's now focused on the kitten as she pets his belly.

"And that's basically it, in a nutshell," I add.

"There's much more to you than just that, Nick," she counters, alternating her gaze between the cat and me.

"Ava," I start, taking a deep breath, "Believe me when I say that I have opened up to you more than I have with anyone else I've only known for a month."

"I understand," she whispers softly.

"What's on your mind, sunshine?"

"You're absolutely right," she says.

"Right about what?" I ask, my eyes looking for hers as she focuses on the sleeping kitten.

"It's just...you've only known me for like a month, Nick," she starts, "You don't really know me, and you don't have any obligation to tell me anything about yourself."

"Ava, it has nothing to do with knowing you for a month or a year," I clarify, "I don't share certain things with anyone, not with you, not with my friends, not even with my family."

"You don't have to explain yourself to me," she says offering me a warm smile.

"What would you like to know about me?"

"You don't have to do that, you know," she says, tilting her head charmingly.

"I know I don't, but I want to. Ask me anything you'd like to know about me, and I'll tell you. I'll even let you know if it's something I don't typically discuss."

"Why are you being so forthcoming now?" she asks.

"Why not? It's a Wednesday night, and I don't have anything better to do."

"And what's the catch?" she asks.

"Ah, there's the rub. In exchange, I'd expect a response to one of my queries to keep things fair."

"You know I'm quite talkative, right? This will be much harder for you. Are you sure you really want to do this?" she challenges me.

"Oh, come now. What harm can it do?" I reply with a shrug of my shoulders, aware that this may not be as effortless as I first expected it to be.

"Right, here we are then," she says, taking a deep breath. "Can you tell me what happened to your brother?"

I was prepared for this question, *in a way*. "He passed away."

"Yes, I had gathered that much," she nods, offering me a comforting smile.

"Would you like to know the details?"

"I would like to know how you feel about it," she says, tucking her legs under her on the sofa and looking at me intently. "The way you react to the topic, especially when Maggie brought it up before and when you told me about how you had to get closer to her after your brother's passing. It's obvious that you are still struggling with it." She pauses, her gaze lingering on me. "Considering he was still young..." she trails off, leaving the sentence unfinished.

"He was exactly one year older than me," I let her know. I take a calming breath and allow myself to sink into the comfort of her sofa's cushions.

"Was he sick?" Ava asks.

"No, not at all," I reply, my gaze shifting away as I seek to sidestep the question.

"Was it an accident, then?" Ava prods further.

"You could say that, yes," I respond, allowing a sigh to escape my lips.

"Involved with a car or a motorcycle?"

I shift my gaze to meet hers and decide to shed some light on the situation. "Do you recall Maggie mentioning her father teaching her how to swim?"

Ava nods in recognition, "Ah yes, I remember. You changed the subject then."

"Indeed, I did," I concur with a nod. "Josh's passing was due to a diving accident."

Ava's expression remains unchanged, filled with her trademark calmness, "So diving was his sport then?" she asks.

"He was reckless and irresponsible, leaving behind his wife and child to face the consequences, yes."

I don't like this.

I am feeling my emotions starting to rise.

"That's why you avoid talking about it?" Ava asks with a gentle tone.

"What do you mean?"

"You are still angry at him," she says, offering me a warm, understanding smile.

"Of course, I am! He took foolish risks, Ava. He was aware of the dangers, yet he went ahead anyway," I exclaim, putting the kitten next to me and rising from the sofa, my voice also rising in anger. "He had a daughter, for fuck's sake! He should have considered the responsibilities he would leave behind."

I realize I am pacing back and forth in front of Ava's sofa as she remains seated, calmly observing me until I have finished speaking. Only then does she rise to her feet, moving to join me.

She halts in front of me, causing me to stop pacing. "Would you like to know what I think?"

I take a deep breath, "Well, what do you think?"

Ava gently places her right hand on my face and begins, "I believe that individuals make decisions. They are not necessarily right or wrong, they are just their own choices. Sometimes, the consequences of those decisions affect others, but that doesn't mean they intentionally wanted to harm anyone. It's just the outcome of their choices." She takes a moment to gather her thoughts before continuing, "It takes time to understand why someone made the decisions they did. It's painful, it might even not ever completely go away — overall, it just takes time."

"Ava, you really need to stop speaking," I tell her calmly, my gaze lingering on her lips.

For real, you are making me want to kiss you, sunshine.

She counters, "And you need to stop avoiding the elephant in the room."

I chuckle, "I'm not avoiding any elephant. That was a terrible analogy."

Ava gazes at me with a soft expression and says, "You have a lot of anger inside of you, Nick."

I give in and ask her, "Do you want to know why?"

Ava nods, "Why?" still holding my face.

"Because anger was easier than tears and way easier than grief," I explain to her, for the first time ever, sharing my feelings about my brother's death with someone.

—

AVA

"I should get going," Nick runs his fingers through his hair. "It's getting late, and you have work tomorrow, and so do I."

"You don't have to leave," I say, hesitation clear in my voice.

Why am I even saying that?

Nick holds my gaze for a moment, and then he repeats, "I really should." He walks toward the entrance of my apartment, his hand resting on the doorknob. He pauses for a brief moment and, without looking at me, says, "Goodnight, Ava."

The door shuts, leaving me alone with the nameless kitten on my couch. Those gorgeous amber eyes are fixed on me. *Shit.* Another set of amber eyes in my life.

Petra taps her stiletto nails on my desk, "So, you got yourself a cat, huh?"

I take her hand, putting a stop to the tapping, and flash a grin. "Yes, I have a tiny ball of fur. He's male, grey, and has amber eyes."

Petra giggles, "Oh my... did you adopt Nicholas?"

I roll my eyes and shake my head. "I said he's grey, Pet."

She grins, pushing further. "But isn't our beloved Nick a morally grey character?"

"I didn't adopt Nick. But I did adopt the kitten because of him."

Petra leans back, "Wait, what?"

"He found the kitten on the streets and didn't know what to do with him, so I took him in," I explain, grabbing my phone to show Petra a photo of the little furball, who's curled up on my lap in the picture. "I haven't given him a name yet. Any suggestions?"

Petra contemplates for a moment before suggesting, "How about Smokey? He looks like a Smokey to me."

"Nah, not quite feeling it."

"How about Sage?" she proposes.

Again, I reject the idea with a shake of my head. "That's not it either. I'm just not feeling any name for him."

Suddenly, Rodrigo appears behind Petra, hands in his pockets and eyebrows raised. "What are you ladies plotting about?"

I hold up my phone, revealing the same photo of the cat that I showed Petra earlier. "We are discussing this little guy."

"When did you get a cat?" Rodrigo asks, confused. "You left work yesterday without a cat."

"I know, it's sudden. But he needs a name."

"It's a boy, right?" Rodrigo confirms.

"Well, you named Saskya, and I like her name. You are good with names," I state.

He ponders for a moment before suggesting, "How about Koa?"

The name sounds nice.

I repeat it to myself. "Koa... I actually like it."

"See? You should have asked me first. He would have had a name from the moment you picked him up from the streets," Rodrigo teases.

Petra gives me a suggestive look. "Oh, she didn't pick him up from the streets."

I raise my eyebrows at Petra.

"You bought him?" Rodrigo asks.

Petra informs him with a nod and a sly grin, "No, it was Nicholas."

"Nicholas, the lawyer?" Rodrigo looks at me quizzically.

I take a deep breath and respond, "No... Nick, the builder... of course, it's Nick, the lawyer."

"What's going on there, Ava?" Rodrigo probes further.

"Nothing is going on. He found the kitten, and knowing I'm a cat lover, he brought him to my apartment," I explain but instantly regret it.

Great job, Ava. You just shared too much.

"He went to your place? Last night?" Petra's voice rises with excitement.

"Oh my God... no, it's not like that." I wave my hand frantically, scanning the area to ensure nobody is eavesdropping, and silently pray for Petra to lower her voice.

"Nicholas Thompson showed up at your place with a stray kitten he found on the streets last night?" Rodrigo asks.

"That's what happened. What's the big deal?" I ask, glancing between Petra and Rodrigo.

"I don't know Nick very well, but he doesn't strike me as the type to pick up stray cats and look for a home for them…" Petra throws her hands up in surrender. "But, what do I know."

"He is not, Bird. He really is not." Rodrigo chuckles.

"You know what, you two are a match made in heaven," I tease, angling my head to the side.

"Thanks, Ava. But let's get back to the matter at hand."

I cut in, "There's no need to bring up the cat anymore. Can we please get back to work now?"

"You know I wasn't really going to talk about the cat, right, Ava?" Rodrigo winks.

"Yeah, yeah. Let's just get back to work," I say.

"Sure thing, boss," he jokes, grabbing Petra's waist and nodding towards the door. "We will catch you later."

"Bye, guys," I call after them.

CHAPTER NINE

NICK

"Rod, if you're ringing me up to give me more high-maintenance customers, my answer is a firm 'no'," I quip, settling into my chair at the office.

"Nah, I just wanted to ask you a quick question: when did you become a cat person?" Rodrigo's voice comes through the phone, and my heart sinks a little.

He already knows about Ava's cat.

"I don't know what you're talking about, mate."

"You gave Ava a cat, Nick. A stray cat. Since when did you start picking up random cats off the street?" Rodrigo laughs on the other end.

"I found it at night, and it looked lost, so I decided to give it a home," I hope this is the end of it.

"Nicholas, Nicholas..." Rodrigo begins, "Did you honestly find the kitten on the streets?"

"Absolutely... do you believe I purposely bred a male and a female cat to give a little one to Ava?" I jest with a composed tone while sorting through some paperwork on my desk.

"Even though I believe you would be the guy to do it, in this case, no, I don't." Rodrigo laughs.

"Anyway, if this conversation's done—" I begin to say, but Rodrigo cuts me off.

"No, hold up. I've got a serious question for you," he says.

I brace myself for what's to come. "What is it?"

"Since when did you turn into such a softie?"

I let out a deep sigh. "Alright, I'm hanging up now," I say, shaking my head as I end the call.

Upon ending the call, I glance at my phone and weigh the possibility of texting Ava. But no, that would be too forward.

What are you even thinking, Nicholas? Are you getting mad?

Rodrigo is onto me. I didn't discover the kitten wandering the streets – nor did I breed it. Instead, I picked him up from a couple who were giving away their kittens for adoption.

As for the fact of the kitten having amber eyes, it was entirely coincidental. When I arrived, only the small kitten remained. No one wanted him, so I took him home.

Admittedly, it was a risk to bring the kitten to Ava before discussing it with her. However, I had to make it appear genuine. I couldn't just confess that I wanted an excuse to be closer to her.

Damn it, Nicholas. Damn it.

I let out a big sigh. What the hell is happening to me? Is Rodrigo actually right? Am I getting soft?

—

AVA

Work's over, and it's finally time to head home and see Koa.

Should I text Nick and let him know that I named the kitten? He did give me the little furball, after all.

No, scratch that. He probably couldn't care less.

The way he bolted from my apartment yesterday doesn't exactly scream 'eager to chat'. I shouldn't have brought up his brother, either. Pushing him to talk about something he didn't want to share wasn't cool. Why do I even care so much about him?

He wasn't always the most pleasant guy to be around. He has this grumpy vibe almost all the time. But there are these fleeting moments when he isn't like that, and those moments... they got me used to a certain way of being around him. So now, when he's a bit cold or distant, it throws me off my game.

Goddammit, Ava. Just...goddammit.

As it's already after 7 p.m., I'm the last one to leave the office, so I lock the glass door with my keys. While I'm closing the door, my phone beeps inside my bag. I try to reach for it, but the door is stubborn.

The phone beeps again.

"Ugh, seriously?" I grumble, finally shutting the door and making my way to my car.

I fish my phone out of my bag, juggling it with my car key as I walk. I see two messages from Nick, and my heart jumps and sinks at the same time.

Nick is texting me? I stop in the middle of the sidewalk, unsure of what to do.

I unlock my phone and start walking toward my car. The first message reads, "Still working, sunshine?" and the second one says, "Just checking in on tiny Nick."

I can't help but burst out laughing in the middle of the street. "Oh, Nicholas... do you even realize how dirty that sounds?"

I quietly chuckle to myself while looking at my phone screen.

"Do you have any idea how that sounded, Nicholas? By the way, I'm just getting in my car now, so I have no idea how Koa is doing." I reply, hiding Koa's name in the middle of the sentence to see if he notices.

"Koa?" he responds, "You named the cat without consulting me?"

"You just called him 'tiny Nick'..."

"I don't see the problem, Ms. Adams," he replies.

I smile as I get into my car, put my bag in the passenger seat, and text Nick before driving off, "Going to drive now."

"Drive safe, love," Nick texts back.

I stare at the message for a few seconds before mustering up the courage to send one last message, "If you want, I will be home in half an hour. You can come over and see Koa."

My phone stays silent. *No notification*. I check my phone screen again, but there's nothing there.

"For heaven's sake, Ava... you've messed it up again," I grumble, banging my head lightly on the steering wheel.

NICK

Did Ava just invite me over?

Yes, she did.

I've been staring at her message for the past ten minutes, unsure of what to reply. *Should I go?*

I slowly get up from my chair, close my laptop, and slide it into its sleeve along with some documents I need to work on. I take them with me as I walk to the door.

As I reach my car, I place everything on the passenger's seat and sit for a few minutes, still pondering what to do about Ava's message.

"You are getting too involved, Nicholas."

Is this really what you want? One week ago, you didn't even crack a smile at anyone, and now you are opening up to a girl about your feelings, past, and personal life? You went to pick up a cat for her...

"Bloody hell." I mutter.

I start up the engine and begin to drive towards Ava's place. *Screw it.* I'm just going to go ahead and keep up with this. I stop by a local pizza joint to grab some dinner and then head over to her flat.

As I approach the building, I notice that the door is already open, so I make my way up to her floor and knock on the door. I can hear a lot of noise and something falling inside.

What on earth is she up to? Is she trying to start a war in there?

"Just a sec!" I hear Ava shout.

Oops, I forgot to tell her I was coming.

Once again, bold move, Nick. Very bold.

Finally, the door opens, and Ava says my name, looking surprised to see me. She's still in her work outfit, with her wavy blonde hair falling over her chest and her mouth slightly open.

"I've got pizza," I tell her, not adding anything else.

"I thought—" she begins to say, but as she speaks, Koa runs out of the flat.

"Koa!" Ava exclaims, and I quickly bend down to catch the cat, holding the pizza boxes in my other hand.

"And a cat..." I joke, "I've got pizza and a cat."

Ava giggles sweetly and reaches out to take Koa from me. "Thanks for catching this little one," she says, tilting her head. "Come on in."

I enter Ava's flat and place the boxes on her kitchen island.

"You know a lot of this could have gone wrong, right?" she asks behind me.

"What do you mean?" I ask, turning back to face her.

"You didn't say you were coming," she notes, "You didn't reply to my text... I could have taken more than thirty minutes, and I could have dinner already."

"You said thirty minutes. Thirty minutes, it's thirty minutes. Unless you didn't mean it when you asked me over."

"Imagine if I wasn't home yet—" she insists.

"I would wait."

"Okay... and I would still be surprised." She replies.

"Do you want me to go, sunshine?"

Honestly, I'm not sure if I should be here. What if she was just trying to be nice when she asked if I wanted to see Koa?

"No!" she quickly replies, motioning in my direction, and then tries to compose herself.

That was cute.

She couldn't hide it.

Shit, Ava... what was that?

"I didn't mean it that way. I want you here," Ava says.

"You want me here?" a smirk escapes my lips.

"I wanted you to come and see Koa. That's what I meant. Stop flipping everything I say around." She crosses her arms in front of her chest.

Yep, she's getting worked up.

Okay, Ava... I like where this is heading.

"Doesn't matter that I didn't reply to you, okay? You said half an hour, and I showed up in half an hour. You were leaving work, and I brought pizza. If you were late, I would wait. If you had dinner ready, I would eat the pizza by myself." I remark.

Ava starts laughing, "No, you wouldn't. I would be eating my pizza and the other dinner."

"Sunshine... Ava... darling," I tease, "Don't insult me. Look at you – you eat like two apples per day, maximum."

"What is that even supposed to mean?" she opens her mouth in shock.

"Your body, Ava—" I start. *Your body is perfect*.

No, no, no... Nicholas. NO!

"I mean that you don't have the body of someone who eats a lot, that's all." I finish my sentence and turn my back to her before I say anything I shouldn't say.

"Okay, Mr. Judgmental," Ava strolls to the other side of the kitchen island to face me, "Let's eat the pizza and see who can eat more slices."

I shake my head, "You are going to regret it."

"Anyway, let's see what pizzas you brought." She reaches for the boxes and opens them to take a look inside.

We are sat on the sofa scoffing pizza whilst Koa runs around like a mad thing. "Are these the so-called 'zoomies'?" I ask.

"Yeah, pretty crazy. Yesterday he was so quiet, but today he's all over the place," Ava warmly replies.

"And yet, you prefer cats to dogs?" I tease her.

"Ha, ha. I've said it before, I'm an animal lover. Dog people are the picky ones," she offers me a smile.

"Dogs can be just as crazy, you know?"

"But you don't have a dog, do you?"

"Nope, but I used to. Had dogs all my life – stopped having them in Seattle."

"Isn't it lonely living alone, though?" she looks at me.

"What do you mean? You were also living alone until yesterday."

"Right," she acknowledges, biting into her pizza and looking away from me.

There's an awkward silence until her phone starts ringing on the coffee table in front of us. I unintentionally look at the screen and notice a name, Jax.

Rodrigo mentioned him. *He's Ava's ex.*

Talk about perfect timing...the universe keeps sending me these signals. The conversation leads to the guy, and now he's calling her.

I don't look at Ava, but I can feel her tensing up beside me. She doesn't reach for the phone for a few seconds, then finally declines the call and puts the phone back on the table. She reaches for the TV remote and turns it on to a random channel.

"Nick," she starts after putting the remote down, "I wanted to apologize about last night."

Our eyes meet, and I ask, "Apologize about what?"

"About pushing you to talk about your personal life." She clarifies, and I find my opportunity in her words.

"You shouldn't."

"How so?"

"I'm not sorry that we talked about my brother yesterday, sunshine." I swallow my pizza and continue, "It means I can still ask you a question about yourself. Remember?"

She closes her eyes slowly and nods in understanding, "I just gave you the perfect opportunity, didn't I?"

"Yes, you did, Ms. Adams. You and that call you just got and declined."

"I declined it because we are having dinner, Mr. Thompson."

"Right, but the name on the screen..." I begin and then leave it hanging.

"Were you peeking at my phone, Nicholas?" she asks mockingly.

"Your phone is on the coffee table, Ava. I just happened to glance at it," I reply, also using her first name to match her tone.

"For all I know, it could be my brother," she says.

"For all I know, you don't tense up at the sight of your brother's name," I raise an eyebrow.

Ava scoffs and finally gives in, "Okay, what do you want to know?"

AVA

I eventually give in, "Okay, what do you want to know?"

He wastes no time and gets straight to the point, "I want to know about your ex-boyfriend, Jax, right? The guy whose name just popped on your phone."

"You assume a lot, don't you?"

He shoots back, "Am I wrong, though?"

With a deep breath, I respond, "No, sir, you are not wrong."

Taking another slice of pizza, he asks, "So what was the deal?"

I adjust myself on the couch and prop my feet up, trying to maintain some composure despite still being in my work skirt. "We were together for a long time, but we broke up recently."

Nick's gaze travels down my legs and back up to my face. "Why did you break up?"

"Getting straight to the point, are we?" I tease him.

"Well..." Nick begins, putting down his pizza slice and turning towards me, propping one leg half on top of the couch, "I'm waiting, sunshine. Don't leave me hanging."

"I discovered that he had a child," I say, attempting to sound casual, but my voice betrays me.

"Child, you say? Boy or girl?"

"Boy. But here's the kicker – the child was conceived right after our first breakup. We were in New York, still together as a couple and best friends, but he left for a business trip, so we decided to part ways for some time until, eventually, there was an opportunity for us to be back together again. All in all, within weeks, the baby was conceived."

"Bloody hell. I'm really sorry to hear that. How did you find out?" Nick asks.

I take a deep breath before answering. "The woman came here with the kid to talk to Jax," I say, my voice low, "She told him he had a son, and he needed to take responsibility for him."

"Shit," Nick mutters. "To this flat?"

I nod. "Yeah, right here."

"You lived here together, right?" he asks, and I nod again. "Have you been in touch?" he asks while avoiding my gaze.

"Not really," I admit, "We talked a few times after it happened, but I have no idea what he's up to now."

Nick's eyes meet mine again. "Do you think this is just a 'second break' kind of thing?"

I shake my head. "No. This is different. I can't trust him anymore, Nick. He hid from me the fact that he was with someone else. And he claims he didn't know about the kid, but it doesn't change the fact that he was dishonest with me."

"I understand."

I look away from him. "And that's not even the worst of it," I mutter. "We were together, but we weren't really together, you know what I mean?"

"I don't. But if you don't want to talk about it, you don't have to."

I take another deep breath. "He wanted to go to New York, and I wanted to stay in Seattle. Since we left New York, we were never really happy together. He had a car accident, and I went to New York to be with him. We got back together, but things were never the same. He wanted me to change my life for him and move to New York, but I didn't want to."

Nick nods, listening carefully. "It sounds like you made the right choice." I look at him, and there's a smile on his lips before he adds, "I don't understand how you weren't enough for him to be happy in Seattle."

"You don't?"

"I don't, Ava. I don't know the guy, but he clearly doesn't deserve you."

My cheeks flush, and I'm thankful that Nick's attention is on the TV screen right now. Trying to cool down the warmth, I bring my perpetually cold hands up to my face.

Nick's eyes remain fixed on the TV as he breaks the silence. "Ava," he begins, "Do you still have feelings for Jax?"

His question catches me by surprise, and I take a moment to gather my thoughts. "Do you mean romantically?" my hands still against my cheeks.

"Yeah," he confirms.

I sigh inwardly and answer, "No, not in that way. I haven't for a while, even before we broke up and the whole situation with the kid came up." Admitting it out loud makes me feel a pang of shame, and I glance down at my lap, avoiding Nick's eyes.

Nick turns toward me, and I can feel his eyes on me. "Don't be ashamed of that," he reassures me, "If you weren't happy in the relationship anymore, it's natural for those feelings to fade."

I chew on my lip, "But I never told him," I confess, "I just kept the relationship going even though my feelings had changed."

"Maybe you were just trying to fix things between you two. It's not your fault."

I lift my head to meet his eyes, "Thank you, Nick," I say softly.

CHAPTER TEN

NICK

This week has been an absolute nightmare. My office is a chaotic mess, papers and files strewn about everywhere. And to add to the chaos, my personal life is in shambles.

Let me break it down – it seems like all my clients collectively decided that this was the perfect week to schedule meetings with me. Now, that's usually fantastic news. But here's the catch – they all chose the same week, leaving me drowning in an overwhelming workload. As if that weren't enough, my family decided that this was the ideal moment to descend upon Seattle.

My parents are currently touching down in the States. Don't get me wrong, I adore them, but their visit couldn't have come at a worse time.

Ella needed me to babysit Maggie. However, with this avalanche of client meetings, I couldn't give Maggie the attention she deserves.

Maggie, being the candid child she is, spilled the beans to my parents during a video call. She informed them that 'Uncle Nick' couldn't stay with her because he was swamped with work and that her mommy had to find a babysitter. Now, my retired parents are staunchly against babysitters, so they promptly offered to jet over to Seattle and take care of Maggie themselves.

While I appreciate their help, I'm also acutely aware that I've been neglecting spending quality time with them. So, I reluctantly agreed to have dinner with them while they're in town.

"Fuck, fuck, fuck! I'm running late." I scramble to shut my laptop, grabbing it in a rush as I bolt out of the office. "You can head out if you want. Just be sure to lock up!" I call back to Hannah, who's probably eager to leave anyway.

"Thank you, Nicholas," she replies.

I rush to my car, feeling utterly disoriented by how time has slipped away. It suddenly hits me that I completely forgot about picking up my parents from the airport. This week has been an absolute nightmare, and I can't fathom how it could possibly get any worse.

I buckle my seatbelt and connect my car's Bluetooth to call Ella, who has bombarded my phone with at least a hundred text messages while it was on silent.

"Hey, where are you?" Ella's voice comes through the phone as I speed toward her house.

"Hey, is Maggie ready? I lost track of time."

"Your parents are almost in Seattle, Nick," she reminds me.

"Yeah, and I lost track of time. Is Maggie ready or not?" I press.

"She's more than ready, and I am too. I need to leave soon, and I can't leave her alone," she says.

"I figured. I'm almost there. I'll pick her up and take her with me to the airport. You leave me the keys, and I'll give them to my parents when I'm with them," I suggest, trying to smooth out the situation.

"Ok, hurry up," she urges.

"I can't go any faster, trust me," I reply, not thrilled with my current speed.

I race to Ella's place to collect Maggie and the house key before heading to the airport to welcome my parents. Fortunately, their flight is running a bit behind schedule, providing me with just enough time to reach the airport before their arrival.

As Maggie and I approach the arrivals gate, I spot my parents waving excitedly in our direction, luggage at their sides. Meanwhile, Maggie is distractedly scanning the area, blissfully unaware of their presence.

"Maggs, look who's there," I nudge her shoulder gently, trying to get her attention.

"Who?" she looks up at me with curiosity.

"Grandma and grandpa," I nod toward my parents, a smile forming on my lips.

Maggie bursts into giggles and rushes toward them, throwing herself into my dad's arms as soon as she reaches them. I follow at a more measured pace, taking in the sight of my parents after such a long time apart.

My mum eagerly approaches me, wrapping her arms around me in a tight embrace. "Oh, my dear son, I've missed you so much!"

"I've missed you too, mum," I reply warmly, returning her hug.

She gazes at me expectantly, "When are you going to visit us more often? You hardly ever come to England these days."

I clear my throat, feeling a hint of discomfort. "Yeah, I know. I need to make more time for it."

I used to visit my parents frequently when Josh was around. We were inseparable, and we'd always travel together. But now, the idea of returning alone just doesn't sit right with me. It might be selfish, but I can't help feeling that way. My folks need me now more than ever, yet even the thought of revisiting those memories without Josh hurts deeply.

I've never been to our family home without him. We both lived in the UK before, but then Ella became pregnant, and we all decided to move abroad – Josh for his growing family and me for my career.

Wherever we went, we went together.

Now, I find solace in burying myself in work to escape the pain of his absence. It also serves as a convenient excuse to avoid visiting my parents. It's a messed-up situation, and I'm well aware of it. My parents already lost one child, and now they're missing out on another because of my selfishness.

They didn't deserve to lose both of us, but sometimes that's how it feels.

—

AVA

Life's been a real rollercoaster this week. Work's been an absolute whirlwind, and honestly, that's the most excitement I've had. Once I'm done at the office, my main mission is to make sure Koa doesn't turn my place into a war zone.

Petra and Rodrigo decided to take a break from the office this week, leaving me to hold down the fort with a bit of help from Pedro. Pedro is Rodrigo's brother and co-owner of the family business along with their dad, Mr. Gomez – *spoiler alert? it's not the same company.*

I know, it might sound like a convoluted setup, but there's this whole merger thing going on between our company and the family business. As a result, some of us are playing double-duty between both places. That's where Petra, who's originally part of Rodrigo's dad's team, and Pedro come into the picture.

After a long day at work, I finally make it back home. Just as I turn the corner to my apartment door, I'm met with the sight of Jax casually leaning against it.

What in the world is he doing here?

My heart starts racing as I walk towards him, my steps deliberate but my mind racing. Jax straightens himself, slipping his phone into his pocket, and greets me with a smile. "Ava," he nods.

I muster a weak smile in return and inquire, "Jax, what are you doing here?"

He remains composed, "I thought you were already home," he responds.

"I had to stay a bit longer in the office. Rodrigo and Petra are on vacation," I explain, reaching for my keys in my white shoulder bag.

Jax steps aside, giving me room to enter. "Always holding down the fort, aren't you?"

I open the door and step inside, but before I can react, Koa dashes out. "For heaven's sake, Koa!" I exclaim, dropping my keys and bag to chase after him. I scoop up the mischievous feline in my arms and head back into the apartment.

"Wait, you have a cat now?" Jax asks surprised.

I glance at him and confirm, "Yes, his name is Koa," as I step inside, expecting Jax to follow and close the door behind him.

"I remember when we talked about not getting a cat because we didn't have time to take care of it," Jax observes.

"Jax, there is no 'we' anymore." I turn around, grabbing my keys and bag from the floor.

"Yet, you still decided to bring a cat home all of a sudden?" His tone irks me.

"I don't appreciate your tone, Jax."

"I'm not trying to judge. I'm just curious."

"There's nothing to be curious about. A friend found him in the streets and gave him to me. End of story." My heart quickens as I mention Nick, even though I refer to him as a friend. I avoid Jax's gaze and head to the fridge for some water.

"Your friend gave you the cat?" Jax repeats.

"Yes, Jax, my friend gave me the damn cat. Can we not do this?" I slam the fridge door shut, gulp down my water, and walk to the couch where Koa is wreaking havoc with my pillows. "So, what are you really doing here?"

"I just wanted to see you. I miss you, Ava," Jax confesses.

"We've been through this before, Jax. You can't keep pushing and expect everything to work out just because you want it to."

"I'm not asking you to take me back. I just want us to be friends again. I want us to have what we once did, even if it's not in a romantic way," he says softly.

"Friends?"

"Yes. The paternity test came out positive. I really am Nathan's dad." His eyes finally meet mine.

My heart pounds in my chest, but it's not the same as if he had dropped this bombshell weeks ago. The truth is, I've been drifting away from this relationship for a while now. His confession is a slap in the face, a betrayal that stings. Yet, oddly, it's also a liberating realization.

"I had already prepared myself for this, Jax. And so had you," I reply with a steady tone. "The girl had no reason to fabricate a lie to you, or to me, or to anyone else. The child is your spitting image, after all."

Jax's admission slips out, "I guess I was hoping it wasn't true."

"It doesn't change a thing between us."

He nods slowly. "Because the reason we broke up wasn't the kid. It was because I kept the fling from you in the first place."

I nod, not saying anything.

Jax clears his throat. "I was wondering if you'd like to have dinner with me. Just as friends. We used to go out in New York before we were even a thing."

"Jax...I don't know," I hesitate.

"It's just a casual dinner, Ava. I'm not asking you to marry me," he quips.

"I don't think it's a good idea, Jax."

"I'll be in Seattle for a few days. How about Saturday at 7 p.m.? Just a casual dinner between friends," he proposes, his eyes filled with hope.

"I don't know, Jax. It's not that simple."

He takes a step closer, making me look up at him, his look intense. "Ava, we can't keep avoiding each other forever. Let's just catch up."

I chew on my bottom lip, contemplating his offer. "Okay. But it's just dinner. Nothing more," I finally confirm, the words escaping before I can fully process them.

Jax grins, relief washing over his features. "You've got yourself a deal."

"Just tell me next time you're stopping by."

"If I did, you would fight me on it," he chuckles, and though I resent his words, I can't deny the truth in them.

CHAPTER ELEVEN

I wake up to the annoying sound of my phone ringing, accompanied by an intense headache. Sunlight streams through the window, revealing a woman I don't recognize lying beside me in bed. My phone keeps ringing, and the woman groans and turns away.

Who is she? I seriously need to cut back on the drinking.

My phone doesn't give up and rings again. I let out a groan before fumbling for it on my bedside table with my left hand. It's Ella, and it's only 10 in the morning. What on earth could she want at this hour?

"What?" I ask impatiently, hoping she has a good reason for calling. There's a pause, and I can hear her sobbing. "Ella?" I say, turning up the volume and holding the phone to my ear while sitting up in bed. "What's wrong?"

My chest tightens as she manages to say, "It's Josh."

My heart sinks. "What happened to Josh?"

"He..." She starts, her voice breaking as she begins to cry again. "He died, Nick."

"What did you say, Ella?" I ask, hoping I misheard her.

"He's gone, Nick. Josh died," she repeats, crying uncontrollably.

I can't even begin to process her words.

My brother...dead?

How is that possible?

Ella continues to cry, and my thoughts are a whirlwind.

"How?" I manage to ask, my voice steady despite my racing mind.

"Diving," she replies quietly.

I take a moment to collect myself before asking, "Where are you?"

"At the hospital," she sobs.

"I'll be there. Text me the details," I say before ending the call.

A hand touches my shoulder, and I startle, forgetting there's someone next to me. I glance over and see a girl sitting on my bed, wrapped in my white sheets.

"You alright?" she asks.

"I need you to leave," I reply coldly. I don't mean to be harsh, but I can't deal with anything right now. I can't think of anything else to say.

She turns away, gathering her clothes from the floor, and I pace around my room, running my hand through my hair.

"It's Hailey," she says.

I stop in my tracks, "What now?" I ask, my tone reflecting my irritation.

"My name," she clarifies, buttoning up her pants. "I'm Hailey."

I take a deep breath and reply, "I'm sorry, Hailey. I don't remember anything about last night, and today is not a good day for small talk." I try to be polite, but it doesn't come out quite right.

Hailey simply puts on her top and leaves without saying a word. I hear the front door slam shut, leaving me alone in silence with Ella's haunting words echoing in my head.

Josh died.

I rush to the hospital, park my car, and hurry inside, dialing Ella's number as I go. She answers almost immediately, and I ask urgently, "Where are you?"

"I'm outside. I needed some fresh air," she replies softly.

"Outside where?" I turn around, exiting the building, waiting for her response.

"I can see you from here," she says.

I spot her holding her phone to her ear, and I sprint toward her, ending the call and tucking my phone into my joggers. "What happened?" I automatically ask as I reach her.

Without a word, she throws her arms around me, sobbing uncontrollably.

"Where's Maggie?" I ask, concerned about leaving the child alone.

"She's with a friend. I couldn't bring her here," she answers between sobs.

"Was he alone?"

"No," she replies curtly, her head still resting on my chest as I hold her. "His friends couldn't get to him in time."

I can't find the right words to say. I just nod and gently rest my chin on top of her head.

Bloody hell, Josh.

—

AVA
NOW

It's Saturday, and productivity is the last thing on my mind today. I've been sprawled on my couch, rocking pastel pink joggers and a cozy sweatshirt, my feet snug in fuzzy socks. Koa, is nestled beneath the blanket, curled up in dreamland. Netflix plays in the background as I indulge in yet another Friends binge-watch session.

I'm in no hurry for this day to end. The prospect of dinner with Jax, given our history, doesn't exactly fill me with excitement.

I mean, he's a decent guy, and despite the kid situation, I don't hold anything against him. Sure, we've had our fair share of arguments, but don't all relationships? Just because a romantic one ends doesn't mean friendship isn't an option.

Part of me bears guilt about this situation. I should have told him that the love I felt for him wasn't the kind I wanted anymore. But I didn't, and it's eating me up inside.

My phone buzzes on the coffee table, snapping me out of my reverie.

I must have dozed off.

Koa's no longer at my side. I rise from the couch and grab my phone, seeing Jax's name on the screen. I'm not in the mood to take the call, so I let it go to voicemail. But there are already three texts from him.

OH NO!

It's 6:30 p.m., and I should be getting ready. I unlock my phone and read his messages: "Hi, Ava! Don't forget about me today," "I'll be there by 6:45 p.m.," and "Ava, did you forget about me?"

No, Jax, I didn't forget about you!

My phone buzzes once more, and I let out an exasperated groan. "Seriously?" I mutter before snatching up the phone. "Yes, Jax. I didn't forget about you, alright? I just fell asleep. I'm in the process of getting ready, and I know you'll be here in fifteen minutes. So, if you'd kindly allow me to shower, dress up, and prepare, that would be fantastic."

"Uh, noted, love," a voice comes from the other end.

Wait, that doesn't sound like Jax. Panicking, I glance at the screen.

It's not Jax — it's Nick.

Oh no, Ava.

"You're back with Jax?" Nick questions, breaking my stunned silence.

"No," I respond abruptly, flustered. "I'm not. I just—"

"It's alright, sunshine," he interrupts, his tone oddly neutral. "I'm not keeping tabs on you."

"I'm not back with Jax, Nicholas," I hurriedly reassure him. Why am I even explaining myself to Nick? My cheeks flush with embarrassment.

"It's alright, Ava," he repeats, unfazed.

Did I want him to be bothered? Why is he calling me?

"Why are you calling me, though?" I ask, attempting to sound casual.

"It was an accident, Ava. I clicked the wrong name, and you picked up right after the first ring."

He didn't mean to call me. Why would he?

"Okay," I reply, unsure of what to feel or say. It's been days since we last talked or saw each other.

"Have a nice supper, sunshine," Nick says before ending the call, not giving me a chance to respond.

I'm left sitting in the living room with Friends playing in the background, my phone still in my hand. Suddenly, a text from Jax appears: "Call me?"

Quickly, I type back, "Sorry, fell asleep. Going to take a shower and get ready fast before you arrive."

—

The doorbell rings, and I'm in the middle of blow-drying my hair. I quickly turn off the dryer and rush to the door, opening it for Jax.

"Hey, pretty," Jax greets with a charming smile as he steps inside.

"Hey. I'm almost done drying my hair. Just give me five more minutes, please."

"Sure," he says, making his way to the couch while I head back to the bathroom to finish up.

After my hair is dry, I apply some mascara and slip on a pair of white Converse to match my light-yellow skirt.

"You'll forever be the only person I know who can put together a nice outfit using yellow," he remarks, grinning.

"Thanks, I guess," I reply, walking over to the entrance to grab my white cardigan from the hanger and my shoulder bag. "Shall we go?"

"Yes, we shall," Jax agrees, getting up from the couch.

"Can you please just turn off the TV while I change Koa's water and check on his food?"

Jax nods, "Sure," before he walks over to the door.

Jax takes me to an Asian restaurant that serves an all-you-can-eat menu. Surprisingly, I find myself enjoying the evening, and I'm not feeling as uncomfortable as I thought I would be.

We reminisce about the old days, talking about what we used to do with Rodrigo back in New York. I was always the youngest of the group, barely an adult when we first met.

"Ava," Jax begins.

I glance up from my meal, taking another bite before responding, "Yes?"

"Thank you for doing this. I really didn't want to lose our friendship. I accept that we are not a couple anymore, but I can't accept losing your friendship."

I nod, but there's something burning inside me, a truth that I need to share. "Jax, I have something to tell you," I begin, trying to gather my thoughts.

Jax sets down his chopsticks, his full attention now on me. "What is it?"

"I wasn't always completely honest with you, and I need you to listen to me as 'Jax friend' and not as 'Jax ex-boyfriend.'"

"Okay, you are low-key scaring me," his expression shifts to slight nervousness.

"It's nothing like what you're thinking about," I assure him.

"I'm not thinking about anything special. I just don't like the tone of where this is going."

"When that girl came into the picture with the kid, she was a bit of an excuse for me to end our relationship," I confess, watching his face for any reaction. He appears confused, prompting me to continue. "I was in a relationship with you, but I don't think I really was in the relationship with you."

"What do you mean, Ava?" he tries to make sense of my words.

"I believe my feelings for you faded over time, even when we were together. All the arguments, all the sleepless nights — something changed inside of me, and I didn't have the courage to tell you. I didn't want to ruin our relationship, so I just kept it quiet. When that woman showed up with your kid—" I pause to gauge his reaction, "—I was actually very mad at you, yes... but something lifted from my body, like a weight I was carrying around. I'm not proud to admit it, and you have every right to be mad at me because it's wrong, and I know it's wrong—"

Before I can finish, Jax interrupts me, "I am not mad at you, Ava." He pauses, closing his eyes briefly and taking a deep breath, collecting his thoughts. "I knew something was off, to be honest. I am not mad, I'm hurt, but I can't also say this was the biggest reveal of my life."

"I am sorry, Jax."

"We both are," he says, leaning back in his chair. "Our relationship was already a bit doomed, wasn't it?" he adds, offering me a weak smile.

I choose not to respond to his question, instead focusing on finishing the food in front of me.

—

NICK

I pace around my living room, muttering in frustration and running my fingers through my hair. "Nicholas, what were you thinking, calling Ava like that?" I scold myself inwardly. It seemed like a good idea at the time, but now I can't believe how foolish I was.

Ava is out having dinner with her ex-boyfriend tonight.

Lately, my evenings have been spent with my parents and Maggie, but tonight they decided to have a night out on their own, and for some inexplicable reason, I assumed it would be fine to call Ava.

Clearly, I was wrong.

What was I feeling? Lonely? Desperate?

What a ridiculous move.

I head to the bathroom, turning on the water. "Nicholas, you are being so ridiculous. Were you really going to use the cat excuse to invite yourself over to her flat again?" I shake my head and peel off my sweatshirt, preparing to hop in the shower.

Ava's words keep echoing in my head. 'I didn't forget about you,' she said. And then the bombshell, 'I know you'll be here in fifteen minutes.' She's going to be with her ex in her flat, a place they used to share.

What am I getting myself into? A love triangle?

I don't do love, let alone triangles.

"This isn't a triangle. It's not a triangle because you're not in love, Nicholas. And she isn't in love with you either." I hold my breath for a moment underwater before taking a deep breath again, trying to sort out my muddled thoughts.

—

AVA

The ride home has been mostly quiet, so I decide to break the awkward silence. "When are you planning to leave Seattle?"

"I honestly don't know, Ava," Jax replies, his eyes still focused on the road ahead.

"You don't know?"

He takes a deep breath before explaining, "I wasn't sure how our conversation would go, so I only booked a one-way plane ticket."

"Wait, were you expecting me to take you back then?"

"It's not that simple," he replies cautiously, "I want us to be friends above all else, but I did have some hopes of possibly fixing things between us."

"That doesn't sound like just wanting to be friends, Jax," I point out, gazing at the passing streets.

"Yes, it is. I wasn't sure where you stood after all this time apart."

"It hasn't been that long."

"Okay, maybe not long, but still. I wanted to understand your feelings, and clearly, they don't align with mine," he admits.

"So, you were expecting me to take you back," I insist.

"For fuck's sake, Ava," Jax snaps, "Yes, part of me wanted you to take me back. But as soon as you said you weren't interested, I locked that idea in a box at the back of my head, alright?"

"What about the kid?"

"I take full responsibility for the kid, obviously," he says. "I'm covering his education and all that. But I'm not forbidden from leaving their side."

"Are they staying in New York with you?"

"Yeah, I'm covering their rent. It was either that or me moving, and I didn't want to move again," he explains.

"You belong in New York, Jax," I offer a bit more softly.

He seems taken aback, slowing down the car and briefly turning his eyes toward me. "Damn, you really don't want me here, do you?"

"I didn't say that," I quickly clarify.

"Well, that's what it sounded like. It's like you're done with me, like we were never friends to begin with, and you just want me to disappear from your life."

"That's not it, Jax," I shake my head.

"Then what is it, Ava?" he pulls over to the side of the road.

"I've been trying to convince myself of something that wasn't real for a long time," I confess. "I'm not sure what I'm feeling right now."

"I didn't do anything to deserve this kind of treatment, Ava," he scoffs.

"I know, Jax, and I'm sorry," I apologize sincerely. "It's not you, it's me. I know how cliché that sounds, but it's the truth. I just don't know what I want right now."

"Alright," he says, turning the car back onto the road. "Let me get you home, and then I'll head back to where I belong."

"Jax, that's not what I meant," I protest.

"Come on, Ava."

"I meant that you belong in New York because that's where you've always wanted to be," I clarify, "We used to argue about it all the time because I didn't want to go back there, but I know that's where you're truly happy."

"I didn't just want to go back to New York," he says, raising his voice. "I wanted to go back with you, Ava. Is that so hard to understand?"

"But I never wanted to go back, Jax," I also raise my voice, defending my position. "I want to stay in Seattle and build a life here."

"And I stayed with you, didn't I?" he asks pointedly.

"But you weren't happy," I fire back.

"No, clearly you were the one who wasn't happy, Ava. So, stop putting that on me," he says, looking away from me and driving on without another word.

Jax parks the car in front of the apartment building, his eyes avoiding mine, and a heavy silence settles between us.

"Jax—" I begin tentatively, but he cuts me off with a sharp tone, "Drop it, Ava."

"I'm sorry," I blurt out, desperate to ease the tension. "I never meant to hurt you."

"I know," he replies.

Taking a deep breath, I ask, "Where are you staying?"

"Hotel," he responds curtly, his gaze still fixed on some distant point.

"Just—" I hesitate, searching for the right words.

"Seriously, don't bother," he cuts in. "I'll be okay. I just need some time to process tonight."

I nod slowly, the weight of our failed conversation pressing on my shoulders. "Thank you for everything, Jax."

"Sure," he says simply, and I realize it's time to go. With a heavy heart, I step out of his car and head home.

CHAPTER TWELVE

NICK

I've been sprawled out on this sofa for who knows how long. I've completely lost track of time. Ever since that unsuccessful call with Ava, my mind has been on overdrive, and I can't seem to shake her from my thoughts.

My brain is in overdrive, and I wonder what Ava might be doing right now. Chances are, she's with Jax in their apartment, rekindling their connection.

And I'm fully aware that it's all my doing, the reason for these swirling emotions. I was the one who let her in, who opened up too much.

My contemplations are abruptly interrupted by the ringing of my phone.

"Hey, Mum," I answer, trying to sound composed. "How was dinner?"

"It was lovely, thanks for asking," my mum responds cheerfully. "Maggie couldn't stop talking the whole time and couldn't stop raving about you."

I chuckle. Maggie can be quite the chatterbox, which is both endearing and challenging.

"She also mentioned a girl named Ava," my mum continues, and I can already sense where this conversation is headed.

Thanks a lot, Maggie. Just what I needed right now.

"Ava?" I repeat, cautiously.

"Well, she said the three of you had a wonderful time at lunch and on your picnic," my mum says, clearly waiting for my reaction.

"Yeah, Maggie and Ava really hit it off," I confirm, my discomfort growing. This is getting awkward fast.

"Is this Ava girl a potential interest, Nick?" Mum asks, catching me off guard.

"I'm not sure what you're implying," I sigh, closing my eyes and sinking deeper into the sofa.

"You know exactly what I mean," she presses.

"There's nothing romantic between Ava and me, if that's what you're getting at."

"Are you absolutely sure? You can always talk to me, love," Mum offers.

"I'm sure."

"Alright then," Mum accepts my answer and changes the subject, "Shall we plan to have lunch together tomorrow, the four of us?"

As much as I value my solitude and freedom from socializing, I genuinely love my parents and Maggie. "Yes, of course. Lunch tomorrow."

Mum then asks, "Could you come and pick us up and drive us to a nice spot?"

"Sure thing. I'll be there by lunchtime tomorrow."

"Great, darling. Sleep well," she wishes me goodnight before ending the call.

—

I sneak into my apartment, being extra cautious not to let my little escape artist of a cat, slip past me again. As I step inside, I head straight for the kitchen, my mind still reeling from the events of the night.

"What a night," I mutter to myself, my emotions a jumbled mess. I pause for a moment, trying to process everything. However, I soon notice that Koa hasn't made his usual appearance. I call out for him, "Koa!"

Silence. Not a single sign of the mischievous furball.

"KOA!" I raise my voice this time, momentarily forgetting that I have neighbors.

Still nothing.

Panic starts to creep in. Where the hell is he?

I begin to roam around the apartment, checking every nook and cranny in my search for Koa. I scan the living room, cautiously approaching the couch, hoping to find him curled up for a nap, but he's nowhere in sight.

I remove all the pillows and blankets, but it's as if he's vanished.

"Okay, calm down, Ava. Where could he be hiding?"

My heart quickens as I realize that Koa is truly missing. I hasten to my bedroom, hoping to find him lounging on my bed, but he's not there either. I gingerly pull back the sheets, half-expecting to see him snoozing away, but the bed is empty.

"Ava, damn it. If you were a cat, where would you hide?" I mutter to myself, the panic intensifying.

I dash to the bathroom, quickly checking the shower cabin and behind the toilet.

No Koa.

Now, I'm worried that he might have somehow slipped outside.

Returning to the living room, I attempt to think rationally. "Where else could he be hiding?"

I inspect under the coffee table, behind the TV, and even inside the kitchen cabinets.

Still, there's no sign of him.

"Come on, Koa, where are you?" I utter aloud, the knot in my stomach growing tighter. The thought of losing him is unbearable. Besides, there's no way he could have left the apartment – all the windows and doors are securely closed.

My heart races as I methodically check every window, convinced that there's no way Koa could have escaped.

This just doesn't make sense. Everything is shut tight.

"Okay, Ava, think. What the hell are you going to do now?" I mutter to myself, feeling my heart racing, a single tear escaping my eye.

I head straight for the kitchen counter, my hands trembling as I grab my phone and unlock it. It's past 10 p.m., and panic sets in.

"Who can I call for help at this hour?" My mind races as I scroll through my contacts, dismissing one name after another.

Maybe Rodrigo? No, he's on vacation with Petra. And the thought of calling Jax after our awkward dinner is out of the question.

"God, Ava, get a grip!" I sob, berating myself. "Think, think, think!" My fingers hover over my recent calls list, and I pause on Nick's name. *But no*, that doesn't seem like a viable option. It's too late to call him now, and I don't want to come across as a total wreck.

I collapse onto the couch as my eyes remain fixed on my phone's screen for what feels like an eternity, my heart pounding. Finally, I summon the courage to press the dial button. There's no turning back now.

—

NICK

My phone lights up with Ava's name calling, and my heart starts pounding.

I stare at my phone screen for a moment, completely caught off guard. My heart races as I see her name flash across the display.

Without a word, I pick up the phone, not sure what to expect. There's a brief moment of silence, followed by her weak voice on the other end.

Is she crying?

"Nick?" she says.

"Hey love, everything alright?" I ask, sitting up straight on the sofa.

"I'm really sorry to be bothering you at this time of night," she begins. Did Jax do something to upset her? If he has, I'll bloody well take him out. "I don't know who else to turn to," she says, cutting off my thoughts.

"What's happened?"

"I don't know where Koa is," she replies quietly.

"Koa?" I ask, confused. "What do you mean?"

"Koa's gone. I came back from dinner, and Koa's nowhere to be found, Nick. I called him, I looked everywhere for him," she breaks down in tears.

"Okay, calm down. I'm sure he's okay," I try to reassure her, already getting dressed to go to her.

"I've checked all the windows, and everything's closed. There's no way he got out. I was there every time the front door opened, and I know he didn't leave the apartment," she says, as I put on my sneakers.

"When was the last time you saw him?"

"I don't know, before dinner?" she replies, uncertain.

"But you're not sure?"

"No," and she breaks down again.

"Alright, love. I'm on my way to you right now. Do you want to stay on the phone?" I ask, grabbing a can of tuna from the kitchen cupboard and making my way to the car.

"You are coming here?" she asks through sobs.

"Yes, I am. And it's non-negotiable."

"But it's late," she weakly protests.

"Yes, and you're panicking," I respond firmly. "Once again, it's a non-negotiable matter, Ava."

"Thank you," she says quietly.

As I drive to Ava's house, I can hear her calling Koa desperately on the other end of the phone at least a hundred times. I park the car and run into the building, jogging up the stairs to her flat door.

I knock twice, and Ava opens the door. She is washed up in tears, her mascara smudged all over her pretty face. As soon as she sees me, she starts sobbing and wraps her arms around my torso.

Shit, compose yourself, Nicholas.

"Hey, it's okay. We'll find him," I try to assure her. "Did you check everywhere?"

She nods, clinging onto me, and I gently place my hand on her back, waiting for her to release me.

She looks up, her tear-stained face glistening in the dim light. I offer a small smile, inwardly rolling my eyes at my own cheesiness.

Nicholas Thompson, the master of grumpiness and dry humor, reduced to a smiling idiot.

"Alright. Shall we go inside?" I suggest, and she nods before turning her back on me and heading in. "You said you couldn't remember the last time you saw him, right?" I make my way to the kitchen counter and pull out the tuna can from my pocket.

"A tuna can?" Ava asks incredulously.

"No, it's a dolphin can," I joke, looking back at her quickly before adding, "I'm kidding, sunshine. It's a tuna can. I didn't kill a dolphin before coming here, I promise."

"Why, though?" she looks at me confused. "You didn't have dinner?"

"Ava, love, I know you're in shock, but bear with me here, please." I walk over to her with the tuna can in my hands, "Cats love fish."

She closes her eyes as if it has just dawned on her and says, "I'm so stupid, for heaven's sake."

"You're not stupid. You're one of the smartest girls I've ever met." I look her in the eye before adding, "Now, let's find your cat."

—

AVA

Nick's voice breaks through the silence, "Where did you look for him?"

"I checked the living room, bathroom, bedroom...pretty much everywhere," I reply, my arms folded in front of me in a feeble attempt to soothe my frazzled nerves.

"Koa! Come here, you crazy cat. I have some fish for you. Stop worrying your momma," Nick shouts.

"I don't know where he could be," I whisper, feeling defeated.

Nick spins around to face me, "We can both agree he's not in the living room. Let's search somewhere else," he suggests.

"Let's look in my room," I say, leading him through the hallway.

"Already taking me to your bedroom, Ms. Adams?" Nick quips, a naughty grin on his face. I feel myself blush at his teasing but simply raise my eyebrow in reply. "Okay, okay. Noted," he concedes.

"I looked for him everywhere, even inside the sheets."

"Did you see him before you left for your dinner?" Nick's expression turns serious.

"I did," I recall, wracking my brain for the last time I saw Koa, "But when I woke up with my phone, he wasn't on the couch with me anymore. I went to shower and get ready, so I'm not sure when he disappeared."

"So, the last time you saw him was when you fell asleep?"

I nod, "Yes, he was sleeping by my side on the couch."

Nick puts his finger in front of my face and motions for me to be quiet, closing his eyes as if he's trying to listen for something. "Wait," he whispers, "He's here..."

For a moment, I feel like I'm in the middle of a supernatural encounter, as if Nick has suddenly become attuned to some otherworldly presence. But then he turns his head and starts walking toward my closet.

"Koa?" he calls out softly, his eyes scanning the room. "Would you mind giving us another meow, little one?" he adds with a smile.

I heard him!

"Oh my God, I heard him!" I exclaim, my heart racing with excitement.

Nick slowly swings open the closet door, revealing a small figure pacing back and forth, meowing loudly. "Yep," he confirms as I gasp in relief. Koa darts out of the closet and straight into my arms, his wild meows now directed at the delicious scent of tuna emanating from Nick's hands.

"Oh, Koa, you little rascal," I coo as I hold him close, feeling the tears start to well up in my eyes. But Koa is too distracted by the tantalizing aroma to care about my emotional outburst, squirming in my arms as he tries to reach for the fish.

With Koa safe and sound, Nick takes charge and strides to the kitchen with the cat in tow, holding the tuna can like a trophy. He places both on the kitchen island and turns to face me, a teasing grin on his face. "Ms. Adams, I thought you said you looked everywhere?"

"I did! I would never have thought to check the closet. How the hell did he get in there? He can't open and close doors!"

"Maybe when you were getting ready for your date, he snuck in without you noticing, and you accidentally closed the door on him. Though I must say, he didn't seem too uncomfortable in there," Nick shrugs.

"It wasn't a date," I quickly correct Nick's assumption but immediately regret it. Why did I feel the need to explain myself to him?

Nick doesn't miss a beat, rephrasing his statement without a blink, "When you were getting yourself ready for dinner with your ex-boyfriend, I meant."

I grit my teeth.

As Nick heads for the door, I panic. "Wait, Nick," I call out, unsure of what to say next, "You could stay a bit longer. It's Saturday, and we don't have work tomorrow."

Nick turns to face me, his expression unreadable. "Why would I stay longer, Ava?"

I bite my lip nervously, feeling my cheeks flush. "Because...because I'd like your company for a bit longer, maybe?" I trail off, feeling foolish for sounding so unsure.

"Maybe?" Nick repeats.

My stomach grumbles loudly, making the decision for me. "It hasn't been an easy evening for me, Nick. I could use some company," I say, looking at him hopefully.

Nick stares at me for what feels like an eternity before finally nodding and, without a word making his way to the couch.

—

NICK

To be honest, I've lost track of time by now. Koa has been frantically running around for what feels like ages, but I have no idea what time it is, and I don't really care to check.

Ava asked me to stay, and because I'm apparently a puppy nowadays, I just did. But I'm not regretting it one bit. We've just been lounging on her sofa, with the TV on in the background, chatting about anything and everything.

Mostly, we've been talking about work, but it's not all dull. She's been laughing a lot, sharing stories about some of the eccentric clients at Rodrigo's office. And for some reason, I feel at ease enough to share some of my own stories with her.

"And since we've been talking about work for a while, let's change the subject. How's Maggie?" Ava asks, walking to one of her kitchen cabinets and retrieving something.

"She's with my parents at the moment, actually," I reply as she approaches me, pauses midway, and holds up two different bags of crisps.

"Plain or salt and vinegar?" she asks, tilting her head slightly.

"Salt and vinegar? What are you, a psycho?" I joke.

"Plain it is," she chuckles and tosses me the bag before continuing, "But did you say Maggie was with your parents?"

"Yep," I tell her, opening the bag.

"Do your parents live in Seattle?" she asks as she sits back down next to me.

"No. They live in London, but Ella needed someone to take care of Maggie for about a week, and I had a ton of meetings to attend, so I couldn't have her with me like last time."

"Is Ella your sister-in-law?" she asks, stuffing some crisps in her mouth.

"Indeed."

"I miss Maggie," Ava admits.

"Do you?" I ask, unsure if I'm surprised or not. They get along pretty well, but Maggie can be a pain.

"I do," she raises an eyebrow, "Why does part of you look in shock?"

"I'm just... I don't know," I shrug, "Maggie can be a huge pain at times, and she talks a lot. I mean, sometimes a break from her can be nice," I tease, giving her a half-smirk.

"You can't live without her," she smiles.

I nod slowly in agreement, "I can't, that's right."

"Are you ever considering going back to the UK?" Ava asks out of the blue.

I look at her, not sure where the question came from, and take a second before replying, "I never thought of that, to be honest."

"But you are so far away from your family, literally on another continent."

"I'm sort of a lone wolf, sunshine. I don't mind being away from my parents. And I have Ella and Maggie here."

"I'm also away from my parents, but at least I'm just a couple of hours away from them if I ever need something," she remarks.

I fix my gaze on her for a moment before asking, "And where are you from?"

"From the United States, Mr. Thompson," she teases

"Yes, Ms. Adams, but which state?"

"I'm a New York girl at heart," she answers, pursing her lips and letting out a giggle.

"Sure, you are," I say with a grin, just trying to provoke a reaction. And boy, do I get one.

"What's that supposed to mean?" Ava demands, mouth agape.

"Nothing at all." I look at her, but her expression is so priceless that I can't help myself. I burst out laughing, a real, genuine laugh that I haven't heard from myself in a long time.

Ava regards me with a curious glint in her eye, as though she's just stumbled upon a fascinating exhibit in a museum. Her warm smile remains firmly in place as she asks, "Have you ever been to New York?"

"Yeah, a few times for business. What about you, did you like it there?"

"It's my home, but in a way, I prefer Seattle," she replies, settling onto the sofa and pulling her legs up to hug them. "I've always wanted to leave the continent, not permanently, just for travel. I'd love to go to Europe. Actually, London has always been on my bucket list," she says, a genuine smile lighting up her face as she rests her cheek on her knee.

"Are you inviting yourself to come with me to London?"

"I wasn't. We both know you wouldn't be able to handle a long flight with me," she teases.

"How can you be so sure about that?"

"You wouldn't survive ten hours on a plane with me. Trust me."

"That's a pretty long flight, indeed."

"You see? You wouldn't make it," she chuckles.

"Would you be singing and humming the whole time?"

"No, but–" she begins, but I cut her off.

"Would you be talking non-stop for ten hours?" I continue.

"No, but I have a sensitive stomach, and I fall asleep easily," she says.

"I don't see a problem with that."

"I'd probably doze off on top of you and drool all flight long," she admits.

"That sounds like a pretty picture," Without thinking, I say it out loud.

There is a moment of silence as we both watch the television. Suddenly, Ava breaks the stillness, "I don't want you to go back to London," she says softly.

CHAPTER THIRTEEN

AVA

I hear Koa's meowing, and my eyes flutter open. I'm lying on my couch, facing the TV, which is off. Koa walks by, his tail brushing against my nose, and I realize I must have dozed off.

Why do I always fall asleep so easily?

The living room is already filled with light, so it must be morning. As I reach for my phone on the coffee table, I notice there's something on top of it. I carefully pick it up, trying not to let it fall on the floor, and see a note from Nick.

"Fell asleep on your sofa with you last night. Had to run. Nick."

I smile as I read the note, and then there's a text from him.

"I would make a pregnancy test just in case, sunshine. We slept on the same sofa, it's a dangerous move."

I reply back, "I'm on my pill, it's okay," keeping the joking tone.

"You would be surprised." He says, adding a smirking emoji.

Wait a minute, did Nicholas Thompson just use an emoji? My jaw drops in disbelief.

Before I can react, he sends another text, "It was a typo. I don't use emojis. Obviously." I burst out laughing at his response.

"Sure, obviously a typo."

"Sorry I had to abandon you after our first night together, but I've got a lunch date with my parents and Maggie." Nick's next text reads, and I am amused at his commitment to the role-play.

"Yeah, disappointed. Ditching me for another date."

"Another date, Ms. Adams?" he responds, and I can feel my cheeks flush.

Shit, that's not what I meant to say.

But before I can correct myself, he fires back, "Were we on a date, Ava?"

I swear, every time Nick calls me by my name, it's like my heart starts doing the cha-cha slide without my permission. He usually has some nickname for me, like 'love', 'sunshine', or even my last name, but when he busts out with 'Ava,' I'm like a deer in headlights. Do I play it cool and act like it's no big deal, or do I freak out and start blushing like a tomato? The struggle is real.

"You tell me, Nicholas," I type, playing along with his game.

"If I say 'yes,' what's your reaction to that?" his response pops up.

What is this guy up to? My heart races, and I struggle to come up with a reply.

Just as I'm about to respond, another text arrives. "No need to answer that. Time for lunch, sunshine."

"Say 'hi' to Maggie for me," I type back hastily.

"My parents say 'hi' too," Nick texts back.

Wait, what?

"What?" I type, completely baffled.

"Joking. I would love to see the look on your face, though." he types, and my cheeks flush.

I take a deep breath, trying to steady myself after that close call. "You are playing a dangerous game, Thompson."

"I like to live on the edge, Adams," he replies.

I roll my eyes and smile. I rise from the couch, and Koa trails behind me to the kitchen. I grab a cold-water bottle from the fridge and gulp it down, attempting to calm my jitters.

I start feeding Koa when my phone rings with a video call. I answer it and hear my parents' voices on the other end.

"Hi, Mom. Hi, Dad," I say, trying to sound cheerful. "How are you guys?"

We chat for a while, catching up on each other's lives, before I finally steel myself to say what I need to say. "I have to tell you guys something," I say, my voice shaking slightly. "Jax and I have separated. He's not in Seattle anymore, and we're not living together."

There's a long pause on the other end of the line before my mother finally speaks. "What happened, Ava?" she asks, sounding concerned.

"It's a long story," I say, hesitating for a moment. "But Jax has a kid now. It happened while we were apart when I was still in New York." I can feel my parents' worry mounting, so I quickly add, "But don't worry about it. Everything is okay now, and I don't really want to talk about it."

My parents are quiet for a moment, and I see them exchanging worried glances. "Are you sure you're okay?" my father asks.

"I'm sure," I reply firmly. "By the way," I say, changing the subject. "I have a cat now. His name is Koa, and he's been keeping me company."

I hold up the cat to the phone, and my parents both make cooing noises. "We miss you, Ava," my mother says softly.

"I miss you guys too," I say, feeling a sudden surge of homesickness. "But I'm doing okay, really."

—

"Uncle Nick, why is your hair still wet?" Maggie asks.

This child is astute beyond her years, and I often wonder if that's to my advantage or not. *Honestly, it's not.*

"I took a shower not long ago," I reply, taking a sip of water that the waitress had already set on our table after sliding my phone into my pocket.

"Why you took a shower before coming to lunch?" she probes further.

"Because I smelled bad, just like you," I tease.

"I don't smell bad!" Maggie protests, furrowing her brow.

I give her a smile and ruffle her hair. "It was a joke, Maggs."

But then, she asks the dreaded question. "Who have you been texting, Uncle Nick?" Her innocent question makes me feel like a guilty teenager caught in the act.

My parents turn their gaze towards me, and I feel their judgment even before they say anything. "You know, I was going to ask the same exact thing," my mum chimes in.

I try to come up with a reasonable explanation. "Ava asked me something, and I was just replying to her. But I told her I was going to have lunch with you, and she asked me to tell you she said hello."

Of course, that was a mistake.

My mum's eyes start sparkling, and I know she's already cooking up some matchmaking plan. I quickly turn to Maggie, hoping to change the subject, but then she asks, "Does Ava miss me?"

"She does," I reply automatically, my mind racing with all the possible consequences of my answer. Maggie keeps asking me how I know, and I keep replying, trying to avoid my parents' looks, especially my mum's.

"Can we go back to visit Ava at work?" Maggie asks.

Maggie, darling, can we talk about something else? I plead internally, but the kid just won't let it go. "I'm afraid we can't visit Ava at work," I tell her.

"Why not?" she persists.

"Because it's her workplace," I remind her, shifting the focus. "Hey, where's the food? Is it coming soon?" I scan the restaurant.

But my mum has other ideas. "You look different today, Nick," she observes, scrutinizing me from head to toe.

"It's just my usual clothes," I tell her, knowing perfectly that's not what she means.

"You look lighter," she says.

"Oh, it's probably from doing cardio." I use humor as a defense.

"What's cardio?" Maggie pipes up.

"It's exercise, Maggs. I've been working out," I explain, hoping to move on.

"Really, Uncle Nick?" Maggie's eyes light up.

"Don't encourage him, Maggie," Mum chides, "He's trying to change the subject because he's hiding something."

"Are you, Uncle Nick?" Maggie asks again.

This lunch is going to drag on forever.

CHAPTER FOURTEEN

AVA

I'm taking my lunch break, and Jax's name appears on the screen. He is calling me. The last time we talked was Saturday when we had that dinner, and things were not exactly perfect between us.

Sitting in the office kitchen, looking at my phone while munching on a sandwich I brought from home, suddenly, a voice startles me from behind, "Hey!"

I turn around to find Rodrigo approaching, "Hey."

"Mind if I join you?" he asks, pulling a chair in front of me.

"Of course not."

As my phone starts buzzing again with Jax's name flashing on the screen, Rodrigo speaks up, "I actually wanted to ask you about him."

"What about him?"

"He mentioned your dinner on Saturday," Rodrigo replies.

"Yeah, it wasn't the best," I admit, pursing my lips and nodding slowly.

"I think you should take that call," Rodrigo suggests.

"Is everything okay?" I feel a knot form in my stomach as I grab my phone.

"Everything's fine, but you might want to hear what he has to say," Rodrigo says with a smile before getting up. "I came here to tell you what he's going to say as soon as you get the call. So, there's no job here for me anymore," he adds with a wink before walking away.

I hold my breath as I answer the phone, my heart racing. "Hey, is everything all right?"

"Hey...um...do you have a second to talk?" Jax's voice sounds unsteady on the other end.

"Sure, it's my lunch break," I reply, finishing the last bite of my sandwich.

"I wanted to let you know that I'm going back to New York," he says.

"Back to New York?" I repeat.

"Yes, for good," he confirms.

"Jax, that's not what I meant when—" I begin, but he cuts me off.

"I know. I had a lot of time to think these three days after our dinner, and I am going back to New York because you were right," he explains.

"What do you mean?"

"I belong in New York, and I was never truly happy in Seattle. And if you went back to New York with me?! That would be the happiest version of myself but probably the saddest of you. And honestly, Ava? I think you were right all this time. We were together, but maybe we weren't really together, and I just didn't want to accept that," he confesses.

I close my eyes, taking a deep breath. "When are you going?"

"Tomorrow morning. Actually, pretty much by dawn," he replies.

I try to keep my voice from trembling as I speak. "Jax, I know everything turned out into a big mess, but I love you. Do you know that? You were, are, and will always be one of my best friends."

"I know, Ava," he says softly. "Can I come by tonight to say goodbye?"

"Sure. Of course, you can. I will be leaving work around 6 p.m.," I reply, my heart aching at the thought of saying goodbye to him.

"I can go to the office, talk to Rodrigo and Petra a bit, and then we can go to a coffee shop or something to say our goodbyes. What do you say?" he suggests.

I nod, even though he can't see me. "That sounds good."

—

NICK

As I park my car in Rodrigo's office lot, Maggie sits in the back, bouncing with anticipation. "You're a handful, you know that?"

"We are going to see Ava! We are going to see Ava!" Maggie exclaims, thrilled to have talked me into bringing her along.

"Maggie, we don't even know if Ava's still here. She could be home," I say, attempting to temper her expectations.

"But we can go to her house," she insists as if it's the obvious solution.

"No, we can't just turn up uninvited." I take her hand and lead her into the deserted reception area. "See? Ava's not here," I sigh, feeling bad for letting her down.

Maggie looks downcast and close to tears. "But I really want to see her!"

Just then, a young woman appears from the back of the office. "Excuse me, are you looking for Ava?"

Maggie responds eagerly, "Yes!"

The woman beams at her and says, "Ava just left for the coffee shop down the street. She took her things, so she's probably headed home after that."

"Thank you so much," I tell the lady.

Maggie and I exit the office, and she pleads, "Can we go to the coffee shop, Uncle Nick?"

"You really are a pain, aren't you?"

AVA

"I really wanted to have things sorted out before leaving for New York," Jax says.

"Me too. I felt horrible after our dinner," I admit, my gaze shifting away momentarily.

"I really think we should think about doing something as the group of friends we once were. Like, Rodrigo loves New York as well. One day, the both of you could go back, and for the sake of the old times, we could do something as we used to," he suggests with a smile, attempting to lighten the mood.

"Maybe we could do that," I reply with a tentative smile, considering the idea.

Jax looks at me, his eyes searching mine. "Ava, I want you to be happy," his words tug at my heartstrings. "I really want you to find your happiness, even if it's not with me."

"I wish you the same," I say softly.

He continues, "I hope you can find someone who will treat you well, who can understand you better than I did, someone who will see the real you even when you don't."

Just as I'm about to reply, my world gets hugged by surprise. I glance down. "Maggie!" Shock and joy collide in me. But how in the world did she find me here?

"Maggs, come here!" I hear Nick's voice, as steady and cool as ever.

I open my mouth to introduce Maggie to Jax, but Nick cuts in. "Maggie, time to go. We've seen Ava." His voice is like ice, and I can see the old Nick, the one who keeps his walls high.

"Nick—" I try to bridge the gap, but he's a fortress of silence.

"I don't wanna go, Uncle Nick. Just got here," Maggie's plea is a small beacon of innocence.

Nick pauses, torn between duty and Maggie's wishful eyes. He extends a hand, the universal signal for 'we're leaving'. "Maggie, I'm not asking twice," he says, unwavering.

Maggie's eyes linger on Nick, a silent conversation passing between them before she whispers, "Bye, Ava..." Her disappointment echoes in my head.

What the fuck just happened?

"Who's that?" Jax nudges me.

"Nick?"

"Yeah, he's jealous. Why?" Jax crosses his arms.

"Jealous? No way," I scoff.

"He's got that 'I'll bury you' look. Trust me, I've seen it. He probably imagined it a few times while standing there," Jax smirks.

I struggle with the idea.

Nick, jealous?

"Go, Ava. I'll hit you up when I'm in New York," Jax says, his tone serious but his smile warm.

"Go where?" My heart starts racing.

"Run, go talk to him. It's clear he has feelings for you, and something tells me you feel the same way. So do us both a favor, chase after him, find out what that was all about, before I change my mind and stay in Seattle just to keep you apart from a guy who isn't me but clearly cares a lot about you," Jax says.

I hesitate, then stand, bag in hand.

"Run, Ava, damn it!" Jax's laughter spurs me on.

With no more second thoughts, I bolt down the street, heart pounding like a drum solo, chasing the enigma that is Nick.

—

NICK

Strutting across the parking lot, I hear Ava's voice slicing through the air like a dagger. "Nick!" She's calling me, but I'm doing my best impression of a guy who couldn't care less.

Maggie's hand is in mine, a lifeline in this awkward sea.

Then, Ava's shout cuts through again, sharper. "Nick!" Maggie's head swivels like she's tracking a tennis match. "Uncle Nick, Ava's on a sprint!"

No need for a detective badge, Magpie.

I nudge her towards the car. Just as I'm about to breathe a sigh of relief, Ava's there, huffing like she just ran a marathon. "What the hell, Nicholas? What attitude was that?"

"Just my usual charm."

She's not buying it. "No! That's not 'usual', Nick."

"Sorry to burst your bubble, sunshine, but it is," I shoot back, trying to walk away.

But Ava's got more fire in her. She plants herself in front of me. "Nick, look at me. I need the truth."

I turn, reluctantly. There she is, flushed and fiery.

Damn, she looks good when she's mad.

"What?" I choke out, feeling like I'm in a pressure cooker.

"Were you jealous?" She hits me with it, point-blank.

I hesitate, feeling like I'm walking a tightrope. "I shouldn't be."

"But were you?" she presses, her voice climbing.

I close my eyes, a brief retreat. "You're not mine, Ava."

"Do you want me to be?" Her eyes are pools of hope and fear.

Hell, this is it.

I'm cornered by my own feelings.

I'm a goner for this girl.

"I suck at sweet talk, Ava," I admit, my heart doing a drum solo.

"Good thing I'm a pro at eye-reading," she quips inches away from me, with a grin that sets my world on fire.

"The issue, Ava," I start, locking eyes with her and feeling the electric space between us, "Is that what I'm craving from you isn't about your eye-reading talent."

Ava's gaze lifts. I'm on the edge of something reckless. "What do you want from me, Nick?" she murmurs.

I shut my eyes, a brief defense. "I want to kiss you, Ava," I confess, my voice a low rumble. Eyes open, I add, "And once I start, I'm not sure I can stop."

"Why kiss me?" Ava's eyes drop to my lips, setting off fireworks in my chest.

I'm floundering for words, heart hammering. "Ava, I—" This is it, the high dive. "I've fallen for you. Hard. Don't ask me the when or the why. It just is." My confession hangs there, a tightrope stretched too thin.

Ava's lips part, then close, her eyes drilling into mine. The silence screams.

Great, Nick, you've screwed it up. She's not on the same page.

She blinks, long lashes fluttering like the wings of a trapped butterfly. I'm tensed, every muscle coiled tight, ready for the sting of rejection. My mind's already halfway out the door, escape plans spinning in my head. But then, in a heartbeat, her hand lands on my shoulder, grounding me.

I turn, and Ava — *beautiful, unpredictable Ava* — surges up on her tiptoes. Her lips find mine, soft and insistent. It's like a switch flip in my world. The noise, the chaos, the doubts — all of it falls away, leaving just her.

I pull her closer, my arms wrapping around her like she's the only solid thing in a spinning universe. Her body fits against mine with a familiarity that screams of destiny. Every cell in my body ignites, a wildfire of certainty that leaves no room for doubt.

I'm irrevocably, undeniably, fiercely in love with her.

Her fingers tangle in my hair, a gentle anchor in the storm of feelings. The kiss deepens, a dance of desperation and longing. I lose myself in the taste of her, in the feel of her against me.

Ava pulls back just enough to catch her breath, her eyes shining with an unspoken question.

I'm in love with her, and I don't want to let go.

—

AVA

"I'm sorry," I stammer, taking hesitant steps backward.

"What are you apologizing for?" Nick's voice is a tether in the chaos, pulling me back to reality. He steps forward, closing the gap I'm desperately trying to maintain.

"Maybe I shouldn't have done that," I manage to say, my voice quivering. The words feel as fragile as glass.

"Kiss me?" Nick's question hangs in the air, a simple question loaded with unspoken emotions.

"I — I don't know if that's..." My words trail off, my heart pounding against my chest. I close my eyes for a fleeting second, gathering my scattered thoughts.

"Listen, Ava, there's something I need to say," Nick starts, his voice steady but laced with something raw and unguarded. My heart skips a beat, bracing for his words. "I don't usually do this sort of thing," he continues, his eyes piercing through me. "I've never felt this way before, never even close. You've... you've changed me, and I can't quite figure it out. It's terrifying, feeling this vulnerable."

I part my lips to speak, but all that escapes is a whisper of his name, "Nick..."

He doesn't break his gaze. "I am not over, Ava." He repeats my name, grounding me in the moment. "I lost myself when I lost Josh. His death turned me into someone cold, someone who couldn't love because love meant pain, meant feeling things I wanted to bury. But then you burst into my life, and it couldn't just be simple, could it? You pushed your way into my thoughts, my heart, and now... now, I can't stop thinking about you. So, Ava, don't apologize for that kiss. There's no turning back, and I wouldn't want there to be. I'm not sorry you kissed me."

His words echo in my mind, a storm brewing inside me. "I'm not sorry I kissed you. I'm sorry that I—" My voice trails off.

"There's no going back now. And I kissed you back, remember?" His voice is firm, insistent. "I can't lose you, Ava, not when losing you would mean losing a part of myself again. You've brought back something in me I thought was long gone."

"I'm not going anywhere, Nick," I finally say, my voice steadier than I feel.

"Do you have any idea how special you are?" He continues, "What you've managed to do?"

"I didn't do anything, Nick. I am a mess." I confess, my voice barely a whisper. Even though I try to maintain a composed exterior, I can feel the chaos swirling inside me.

"That's where you're wrong." Nick shakes his head slightly, his eyes holding mine with a kind of gentle intensity. "You always have the right words for me. Always have."

"What if I'm not right for you?" The question slips out, vulnerable and raw.

Nick chuckles, throwing his head back slightly, "Ava, have you ever considered that maybe I'm not the right guy for you?" His amusement fades into a more serious tone. "I mean, look at me. I've never been 'relationship guy'. Never really cared enough to get to know anyone I was with. And the numbers... well, they're not exactly something to be proud of."

"What now?" I ask, wrapping my arms around myself.

"I don't know, Ava... I really don't know how this works."

I offer a small, almost hopeless smile. "Well, you're talking to the girl who's only had two relationships in her life. One before she turned eighteen and the other with her best friend. I don't even know the difference between the two types of love."

Nick takes a deep breath. "Okay, then. The guy who's only had physical relationships and the girl who dated her best friend." He pauses, his eyes searching mine. "Let's go with something cliché, shall we? I don't know where we're going, but we're going there together. Does that work for you?"

"Are you by any chance suggesting..."

"Ms. Adams, I'm not suggesting anything," he smirks, "I just need you to have patience with me. I'm still figuring out this... jealousy thing."

"Nah, not noticeable at all," I tease back.

Nick glances over his shoulder, his eyes drifting to Maggie waiting in the car. "And I'll have to deal with that and with my parents. Maggie probably saw the kiss and will have a field day with it when I get her home."

I laugh, imagining the scene. "You're going to have a great time explaining that to your parents."

He chuckles, the sound warm and genuine. "I will... but I'm sure Maggie will be a big help."

I laugh at the thought.

"Yeah, so much fun," he jokes. "I'll text you, okay? After the interrogation session at home."

"That works."

Nick steps closer, his presence enveloping me. He looks down into my eyes, and then gently presses a kiss to the top of my head. "Later, love," he whispers, before turning and walking back to the car.

Watching him walk away, I realize something – despite the chaos, the uncertainty, and the fear, there's a part of me that feels more alive than ever. Nick and I are stepping into unknown territory, but somehow, it feels like the only place I want to be.

CHAPTER FIFTEEN

NICK

As the car hums down the street, Maggie's voice floats from the back seat, innocent yet probing. "Uncle Nick, did you and Ava kiss?" I grip the steering wheel tighter, hoping the road ahead might offer an escape from her question. But Maggie is relentless. "Are you and Ava boyfriend and girlfriend?"

I take a deep, steadying breath, the words feeling heavy on my tongue. "No, Maggs. Ava and I aren't boyfriend and girlfriend." The truth is, I'm as lost as a ship in a storm when it comes to defining what Ava and I are.

"But Uncle Nick, only boyfriends and girlfriends kiss each other," she insists. *Child's logic.*

"Well, that's not entirely true," I start, immediately regretting the words. I've opened a can of worms, and there's no closing it now.

"I can kiss anyone on the lips, Uncle Nick?" Maggie's questions.

"No, you can't," I reply quickly, a bit too sharply. "It's not like that, Maggie."

Her reflection in the rearview mirror is all big, sad eyes. "Uncle Nick, are you mad at me?"

"No, of course not, Maggs."

"But you sounded mad before." Her voice is small, a mirror to my guilt.

Damn it, she's right.

I lost my composure back at the coffee shop with Ava and Jax. "I was, and I'm sorry about that. I didn't mean to talk to you like that."

"Then why did you do it, Uncle Nick?" Her innocence is a spotlight on my behavior.

I exhale deeply, the words painful to admit. "Because I was mad at something else, Maggie."

"What?" Her curiosity is endless.

"Nothing special," I deflect, but Maggie's not easily dissuaded.

"Were you mad at Ava?" she asks further.

I shake my head, even though she can't see it. "No, I wasn't."

"Were you mad at her friend?" Her questions are like a relentless tide.

My patience frays. "Maggie, can you please stop with all the questions?"

"Sorry, Uncle Nick," she murmurs, turning away to stare out the window.

As we pull into the driveway, another realization hits me like a sucker punch. I promised my parents I'd cook dinner tonight, and they're flying back to England in a few days.

I glance at my watch, a sinking feeling in my stomach. They'll be here in less than an hour, and I haven't even checked if I have what I need to make a decent meal.

Smooth move, Nicholas.

I scour every cabinet and inch of my fridge, desperation mounting with each empty shelf. As I feared, I'm running low on everything. Typical me – the guy who never bothers to cook, always relying on the convenience of takeout.

FUCK!

"I want food, Uncle Nick," Maggie pipes up, her small voice slicing through my internal rant.

"It's not dinner time yet, kiddo," I tell her, trying to sound calm.

"But I'm so hungry," she insists, her voice edging towards a whine.

"Have a look in the cupboards, maybe you'll find something," I suggest, knowing it's a long shot.

Her eyes light up with mischief. "Can I have cookies before dinner?"

Oh no, I can't let her have cookies.

"No, sorry, Maggs. Not a good idea before dinner."

"Is dinner going to take a long time?" she asks, her small face scrunching up.

I run a hand through my hair, "I don't even know what we're going to have for dinner."

"Are you going to cook?" Her question is innocent, but it stings.

"I was supposed to, but got distracted with our visit to Ava. We didn't get back in time to make anything."

Then, Maggie's face brightens. "Can we have Bolognese, Uncle Nick?"

She's a clever girl, and the idea hits me like a lifeline. *Bolognese it is.* I'll just order it, and my parents will be none the wiser.

"Great idea, kiddo," I say, relief washing over me as I pull out my phone to order some pasta.

"Yay!" Maggie's cheer is infectious, her excitement bubbling over as she jumps up and down. "We are having Bolognese!"

I chuckle, watching her dance around the kitchen with childlike glee. As I place the order, a small smile finds its way to my face. "Yes, we are having Bolognese."

———

The doorbell rings, and it's my parents. Thankfully, the food arrived just before them, sparing me the embarrassment of an empty dinner table.

As they step inside, the scene is pure chaos. Maggie, a tiny tornado of energy, is darting around the room. My mum, ever the picture of grace, greets her with a warm, indulgent smile. "Hello, Maggie. Did you have a good time with Uncle Nick?"

Panicked, I dart to the fridge, feigning busyness with drinks. Maggie's ability to keep secrets is as reliable as a sieve holding water – which is to say, not at all. I need to derail this conversation before it's even begun.

But Maggie, blissfully unaware of my internal turmoil, pipes up with the enthusiasm of a child who's just discovered a new toy. "We went to see Ava!" she exclaims.

My heart plummets.

Here we go.

Mum's eyebrows arch in intrigue. "Oh really? And what did you and Uncle Nick do?"

Desperate for any diversion, I butt in. "Mum, would you like white wine or water?"

She opts for wine, but her interest in Maggie's tale hasn't waned. As I pour the wine, she turns back to Maggie. "So, what were you saying, darling?"

Maggie pauses, looking thoughtful, and for a moment, I dare to hope we might avoid the impending disaster. Then, like a cannonball blasting through my defenses, she declares, "Oh, Uncle Nick and Ava kissed!"

FUCK MY LIFE.

I'm frozen, holding my breath, my eyes squeezed shut, unable to face my mum's scrutiny. The soft creak of the sofa signals my dad's sudden interest, and my heart momentarily ceases its beat.

Why did I even think bringing Maggie along today was a good idea?

"They did?" Mum's voice holds a note of surprise, edged with something I can't quite place.

"Yeah," Maggie replies, her innocence in stark contrast to the weight of her words.

"Nicholas?" Mum's voice is a blend of curiosity and amusement.

Turning, I face her, my expression a mask of feigned indifference. "Yes, mum?"

"Do you have anything to say to me?" Her smile is small but knowing.

"No, ma'am," I reply, returning the smile with a strained one of my own.

Maggie, oblivious to the tension, continues. "Uncle Nick was mad when we went to see Ava." Her words land like a grenade in the quiet room.

I shoot her a look sharp enough to slice through steel. "Stop talking, Maggs," I say, my smile more a bared-teeth grimace.

"Why? Let the kid talk," my dad says, his voice casually rolling in from the sofa.

Fantastic.

As if Mum's subtle prodding and Maggie's revelations weren't enough, now Dad's thrown his hat into the ring.

"I give up," I mutter, the words barely audible, a white flag raised silently within the confines of my mind. Every muscle in my body is coiled tight, braced for the onslaught of inquisitive glances.

Mum, ever the astute observer, presses on, her tone gentle yet insistent. "Are you telling me then?" Her eyes, sharp and unyielding, seek answers in my every gesture.

I deflect, grasping at the straws of normality. "There's nothing to tell. Let's have dinner, please?" My voice betrays a hint of desperation, a plea to retreat from the edge of this conversational cliff.

But then, like a sudden break in storm clouds, Maggie's voice pierces through the thick atmosphere. "Yay! Bolognese!" Her exuberance is a beacon of innocence, blissfully oblivious to the emotional maelstrom she's unintentionally unleashed.

—

AVA

Striding into my apartment, I'm met with the enthusiastic welcome of Koa.

My mind is like a pinball machine, thoughts ricocheting off every corner, trying to make sense of the wild ride today's been.

Nick and I? We're like two books from different genres trying to write a story together. He's Mr. Never-Had-A-Real-Girlfriend, and I'm Ms. Been-There-Done-That-With-The-Heartbreak-To-Show-For-It.

Settling in for the night, I indulge in the kind of shower that washes away more than just the day's grime, throw together a salad that's more art than food, and cater to Koa like he's royalty.

I'm just about to dive into my culinary masterpiece when my phone decides to throw a wrench in my peaceful evening. It buzzes with an "SOS" from Nick. I shoot back a question mark, and his reply comes quick, "Dinner with parents."

"And Maggie?" I text, a smirk playing on my lips.

"And Maggie..." Cue the soap opera. Before I can even craft a witty response, another text flashes across my screen, "Too many questions were asked... too much seen..."

I burst into laughter. Only Nick could turn a family dinner into a spy thriller. "Drama queen," I type back, my fingers flying over the screen.

"Try meeting my mum and explaining why Uncle Nick and Ava locked lips!" He shoots back, accompanied by an emoji that's grinning but definitely sweating.

"Okay, you win," I concede, still chuckling. Nick, dealing with parental interrogation and a mini-inquisitor in Maggie? That's a sitcom episode waiting to happen.

Nick's texts go silent, and I figure he's neck-deep in family drama, trying to wiggle his way out of whatever Maggie spilled.

Then, twenty minutes later, my phone lights up again, "Maggie told mum I didn't cook the Bolognese."

I blink at the message. *What?*

"Context, Nick. I need context," I type back.

His reply is swift. "Was supposed to play chef. Ordered in instead."

"And why, pray tell, did you order?"

"Got a bit... busy with you, remember?" His message winks at me, followed by, "Kinda slipped my mind, the whole cooking gig."

"So, you cook?" I tease.

"Ms. Adams, I am a man of many talents."

"No doubt about that."

"If you don't hear back from me in thirty minutes, just know it's been real," he texts, the drama dripping from every word.

"Noted, Mr. Thompson."

I finish my salad, but my mind's a whirlwind of Nick and 'us'. What did he tell his parents about that kiss? Are we even an 'us'? My thoughts are a tangled mess, and impulsively, I text him: "We need to talk."

"Breaking up with me before we even start? Ouch." I can almost hear the half-joke in his voice.

"No, about us starting, actually."

"Friday night. I'm picking you up. It's a date," he sends.

"That's not what I meant."

"But that's what I meant. You. Me. My place. Dinner."

"On the menu? Bolognese?" I can't resist the tease.

"Nope. I'm cooking this time."

"Really? Don't you have, like, a job?"

"Perks of being the boss. I clock out early for you," his message reads, making me smile.

"I'm expecting culinary fireworks."

"Prepare to be amazed. I've got skills," he boasts.

"Can't wait to try your tagliatelle," I challenge.

"Truffles included," he promises, setting the bar high.

—

NICK

Post-family dinner, my kitchen looks like a battlefield. Dishes are piled up, screaming for attention. I can't just leave them be — that's not my style. So, I'm up late, scrubbing and cleaning like some kind of dishwashing ninja.

Control freak? Maybe. But I prefer 'enthusiast of cleanliness'.

And let me tell you, this isn't just your everyday cleanup. One of the plates — Maggie's plate — it's like a crime scene of food. Sauce everywhere, bits of dinner clinging on for dear life. And the kitchen island? It's as if a culinary hurricane hit it.

Waking up the next morning feels like crawling out of a cave. I fumble for my phone, squinting at the blinding screen. A quick check of my calendar brings a surprise — *no meetings*. A free day? Well, that's as rare as a unicorn sighting.

I dial up the office, still half-asleep. "Thompson Legal Services, how can I help you?" That's Hannah, always chipper.

"Morning, Hannah. It's Nick. I'm playing hooky this morning. Maybe the afternoon, too. If clients pop in, just play Tetris with my schedule, will you?" I say, trying to sound more awake than I feel.

"Sure thing, Nick. Anything else?" Hannah's all efficiency.

"That's it. You're a star, Hannah." I hang up and stumble out of bed, heading for a much-needed shower.

The hot water's beating down on me, and my mind drifts to tomorrow's date with Ava.

A date. An actual date.

This is uncharted territory for me. What's the protocol here? Do I buy flowers, make small talk about the weather? All I know is I like her – *a lot*. And I don't want to screw this up.

So, the game plan – hit the store for some top-notch dinner ingredients, pick Ava up from work without being late, and try not to be a complete disaster.

Sounds easy, right?

Right.

After toweling off and throwing on some clothes, I grab my car keys and roll up to Rodrigo's office. And no, it's not to see Ava – *plot twist.*

Walking in, I notice Ava's absence at reception. Perfect timing – I'm here on a secret mission about her. I waltz upstairs, memories of Ava playing gatekeeper on my first visit dancing in my head.

I give Rodrigo's door two sharp knocks and catch his eye through the glass. He waves me in with a quizzical look.

"Hey, Rod! Need your help." I stride in.

Rodrigo stands to meet me, "What's up? Nicholas Thompson asking for my help is a headline in itself."

"It's personal, not business," I say, pulling up a chair.

He leans against his desk, eyebrows raised. "Should I be worried?"

"You're shakin' in your boots already, mate," I quip, a grin tugging at my lips.

"Guilty as charged. So, what's the deal?"

"It's about Ava," I dive right in, no beating around the bush.

"Ava?" Rodrigo echoes.

"Yeah, got a date with her tomorrow. Save your comments – I know what you're thinking."

"I'm not shocked, actually. Not even a bit," Rodrigo replies.

"Great, because I need your help."

He smirks. "What could the legendary Nick Thompson possibly need from me in the dating department?"

And there's the punchline. "Exactly that – I'm clueless about actual dating. I'm good with the chase, not so much with the catch."

Rodrigo's smirk shifts into a full-blown grin. "Never thought I'd see the day," he says, amusement in his voice. "Alright, spill. What do you need?"

I take a deep breath. Here goes nothing – asking for dating advice. Who would have thought?

CHAPTER SIXTEEN

AVA

Here I am, sprawled in bed like a train wreck. My throat's a blazing inferno, my ears are throbbing like they've got their own heartbeat, and my stomach? It's doing flips.

Pure, unadulterated agony.

I shot Rodrigo a text earlier, basically a pitiful SOS, "I'm not feeling very well. Won't make it to the office in the morning." I need more than a snooze button to shake off this nightmare.

Last night was a horror show. I was up hugging the porcelain throne, puking my guts out. Sleep was a distant dream, thanks to my throat feeling like it'd been sandpapered.

The office? Yeah, that's a big fat no-go right now.

Rodrigo's text blinks at me from my phone, "Just rest. Don't bother coming in at all. I'll survive."

I don't even text back. Passed out for thirty, and now I'm battling just to get vertical.

Finally dragging myself out of bed is like scaling Everest. Dizzy doesn't even start to cover it. As I stagger to the bathroom, Koa's wailing for his breakfast.

"Not now, Koa. Mom's dying here," I grumble, splashing cold water on my face like that's going to fix anything.

I'm burning up. Just great. Koa's still howling, and I'm a hot mess – *literally*. Every inch of me aches like I've gone ten rounds in the ring.

Panic sets in, and I crumple to the floor, tears streaming.

"Get a grip," I tell myself.

I haul myself up, every move a Herculean effort, and grab my phone. Fingers trembling, I tap out a message to Rodrigo, "Running a fever. Death's doorstep. Can't come in at all today. Sorry."

No sooner do I hit send, my phone erupts into life. It's Rodrigo, and he sounds concerned. "Hey, do you need anything?"

I'm a mess, tears streaming down my face. "No. I don't know. I'm a wreck," I blurt out, barely audible over Koa's insistent meowing.

"Are you crying? Do I need to drag you to the ER?" Rodrigo's voice sharpens with worry.

"No ER. It's just... Koa's on a meowing marathon, everything's aching, and I'm fresh out of painkillers. I want to sleep, shower, but standing feels like an Olympic sport," I sniffle into the phone.

I hear the buzz of office life behind him. "Ava," he starts, but I cut him short, swiping at my tears.

"Don't sweat it, Rodrigo. I'll live. It's just sleep deprivation playing games. I'm heading back to bed."

"You sure?"

"One hundred percent. Sorry for the raincheck today."

"Ava, don't ever apologize for being sick," he says, his tone warm yet firm.

I hear some background noise, and then add, "Don't miss me too much, huh?" I attempt a joke, a weak chuckle escaping me.

"That's asking the impossible. Just focus on getting better, okay? And don't even think about the office tomorrow."

"We'll see how it goes," I reply, ending the call and collapsing back onto my bed.

—

Rodrigo's phone cuts through the air, his eyes darting to the text. "It's Ava."

I lean back, casually observing.

"She's a bit off her game — a bit sick, I think. Had a rough one last night," Rodrigo explains, his fingers already flying over his phone, hitting the call button. "Hey, do you need anything?"

I watch Rodrigo's face shift from casual to concern, and it sets off alarm bells in my head.

I thought Ava was just lost in some corner of the office, not sick at home.

"Are you crying?" Rodrigo's voice sharpens. My anxiety ratchets up a notch.

What the hell's going on?

I can't stay put, rising from my chair, my voice a whisper. "What's with the tears? Is she okay?"

Rodrigo's giving me nothing but silent nods, his focus glued to whatever Ava's spilling on the other end. "Ava," he says, a cryptic one-word response.

I can't stand this cloak-and-dagger routine. "Rodrigo, talk to me. Does she need help?" My voice rises.

But he's like a vault, all locked up. I'm about to explode with impatience. Why can't he just scribble a note or something?

"You sure?" his tone is soft as silk. I'm pacing like a caged animal, feeling useless as Rodrigo gets swallowed up by whatever crisis Ava's dealing with.

That's it. I can't just stand here twiddling my thumbs.

Charging out of Rodrigo's office, I'm all but a blur. The hallway's a mere streak as I make a beeline for the exit, car keys gripped like they're my lifeline.

I'm racing to Ava's pad, no time for beating around the bush. Every second counts, and Ava, she's out there probably needing a knight in shining armor.

Well, guess what? I'm suiting up.

Ava needs someone, and damn it, I'm making sure that someone is me.

———

AVA

I'm sprawled on the floor with Koa finally snoozing on my lap, when the doorbell crashes through our calm bubble. I haul myself up, muscles screaming like I've just survived a CrossFit challenge.

"On my way!" I shout, dragging myself to the door.

Reaching the door, I'm met with the sight of Nick, looking like he just stepped out of a GQ magazine. Great, I'm here looking like a trainwreck in the wake of his polished charm.

What's he doing here on a workday?

"Hey, love!" he greets me, scooping me into a one-armed hug while shutting the door with his other hand. "How you holding up?"

I'm still trying to get my bearings. "Nick? What are you doing here?"

"I came to play nurse," he says, tucking a loose strand of hair behind my ear.

"How did you even know I was sick?"

"Caught your cry for help at Rodrigo's," he says, connecting the dots for me.

But as I try to stand, the room starts spinning. "Nick, I feel awful," I confess.

His hand finds my forehead. "You're burning up, baby. Let's get you to bed."

Baby.

In the background, Koa's meowing up a storm, reminding me of my duties. "I need to feed Koa, and his water–"

"Shh, I've got it. You, bed. Now," he insists, gently guiding me towards my bedroom.

I just nod, too weak to argue.

Halfway there, Nick smirks at me. "This pace is killing me, grandma," he teases, then scoops me up in his arms, fireman-style.

As he carries me, my heart does a funny little skip. Is this actually happening? Nick, carrying me to my bed?

He gently lays me down, and I ask, "Shouldn't you be at work?"

He raises an eyebrow, his smirk growing. "You kicking me out already, Ava?"

I quickly shake my head. "No, it's just... I don't want you missing work because of me."

He chuckles, a sound that's oddly comforting. "Ava, my name's on the building. I think they'll manage without me for a day."

I let out a reluctant laugh. "Okay, you win."

"There's a good girl. Now close your eyes, rest up. I'll feed the little king and dash out to grab you some meds," he says, already heading towards the door.

I close my eyes, letting the darkness take over.

—

Armed with Ava's keys, I make a quick dash to the pharmacy for her meds. When I return to her place, it's so quiet you could hear a pin drop.

Slipping into the bedroom, I spot Koa dozing at the foot of the bed. Ava's curled up, looking fragile and small.

Damn, sunshine, you really know how to tug at my heartstrings.

I tiptoe over, not wanting to startle her. Gently, I run my fingers through her hair, hoping to wake her up without scaring her half to death. Her eyes flutter open like butterfly wings.

"Hey," I say, brandishing the meds and water like a trophy. "Got you some relief."

She barely manages a hoarse whisper, "My throat—" it's clear talking's a big task for her right now.

"I got you, baby. A buddy of mine hooked me up with the perfect cocktail for this. Pills and lots of water, okay?"

She gives me this tiny, frail nod, and I help her sit up to take the medicine. "I'm sorry."

"Sorry for what?" I ask, "Being sick? You're not making any sense."

"I'm too much work," she whispers.

I crack a smile. "Don't worry about it. I'm a bit of a workaholic," I joke. Her smile, weak as it is, lights up the room.

She takes the meds and gulps down the water, but then she just sits there, lost in thought.

"You okay, sunshine?" I check her forehead again, still worried about her fever.

"Can you lay down with me, Nick?" she asks, and I swear my heart does a backflip.

Get a grip, Nicholas – she's asking for a cuddle, not a ring.

"Sure," I manage, my voice steady.

She shifts to her side, and I kick off my shoes, sliding in beside her.

Bad idea, Thompson. She's burning up and here you are, mind in the gutter.

She breaks the silence. "Mind hugging me?" she asks, noticing my hesitant arm.

I wrap my arm around her. "Like this?"

Her voice is faint, "You never did this, did you?"

Busted. "No, not really."

"Well, Nicholas," she says, her voice gaining a bit of strength, "I hope you're into cuddles, because I'm a big fan, and this is going to be a regular thing from now on."

Your command is my wish, sunshine.

—

AVA

Waking up in Nick's arms is like waking up in a warm, safe cocoon. I sneak a peek at the clock – wow, we've been out for hours.

I try to shift without waking him, but no dice. His eyes flutter open, locking onto mine.

"Morning, sleeping beauty," he murmurs, voice rough with sleep.

"Hey," I respond, a smile playing on my lips.

He pulls me in, his face buried in my hair. "How you feeling?"

"Better, but still a bit like I've been hit by a truck," I admit, my body aching slightly as I breathe.

He nods, his hand drawing comforting circles on my back. "Was worried about you," he confesses, his voice soft.

I nuzzle closer, "Thanks for playing nurse," I say, my voice muffled against his chest.

He responds with a gentle kiss on my forehead. "Always," he whispers.

We're quiet for a beat, then I gather the courage to bring up what's been on my mind. "Nick?"

"Yeah?" He looks down, his expression open.

"I need to talk about us. About what we are," I start, my heart pounding. "I don't want to rush, but I don't want to just drift aimlessly either."

He frowns slightly, but his eyes are kind. "I get it," he says. "I'm not looking to rush things, but Ava, I know I want you. Just you."

His words send butterflies racing in my stomach. "I want that too," I confess, "But I'm scared."

His hold tightens, "I know. Me too. I've never felt like this before. The last thing I want is to hurt you."

Tears well up, and I hide my face in his chest. "I don't want to hurt you either," I whisper.

There's a pause, and then I voice a fear that's been nagging me. "What if I can't always be honest? Like with–"

"Jax?" His voice is gentle, "It's okay to say his name. I know I flipped out before, but he's part of your life, and I need to accept that."

"What if I struggle with honesty like I did with him?"

His answer is simple, "We promise to always talk it through. No matter what. Deal?"

"Deal," I whisper. "Honesty. Always."

He seals our promise with a soft kiss. "I'm glad," he says, his breath warm against my skin.

—

NICK

Ava's out like a light on my chest. Glancing at the clock, I realize it's way past lunch, and meds on an empty stomach? *Not on my watch.*

I slip out of bed ninja-style, trying not to wake Sleeping Beauty. Koa, the furry alarm system, leaps off the bed and darts to the living room, signaling it's chow time.

In the kitchen, I hover in front of the fridge. Raiding Ava's supplies without asking feels like I'm crossing a line, but waking her up for a green light seems worse. Time to make do with what I've got.

Spotting leek, celery, chicken stock, and chicken breast, it's like a lightbulb goes off.

Chicken soup – Mum's secret weapon against all illnesses. *Just one problem – no whole milk.*

Looks like it's time for some culinary improvisation.

I line up the ingredients like a soldier prepping for battle. Operation Soup is a go.

Fast forward, and the kitchen smells like I've just conjured up a miracle. Ava shuffles in, looking like she's been through the wringer. "What's that amazing smell?" she asks, her voice weak but curious.

"You need to be resting," I say, rushing over to her, hands supporting her waist like she's made of porcelain.

"I'm sick of the bed," she protests, giving me those irresistible puppy eyes.

Fuck, she's good at that.

"But you need to heal," I insist, drowning in those big, beautiful eyes of hers.

"What's cooking?" she sniffs the air.

"Chicken soup."

"You made chicken soup?" She looks at me like I've grown a second head. Should I be flattered or offended?

"Yep. Told you I'm a man of many talents," I tease, winking at her.

"I had ingredients for chicken soup?" She's still processing this.

"Yep. But you were missing whole milk. And nutmeg."

"Nutmeg?" She's totally lost.

"Nutmeg, you know, the secret spice of life." She winces slightly, pain still etched on her face. "Let's get you comfy on the sofa. What do you want to watch?"

"Wow, Nick Thompson playing nurse and chef?" She's beaming now, and it's worth every effort.

"This isn't special treatment, Ava. It's just how you deserve to be treated," I flirt, watching her cheeks turn a shade of pink. "Pick whatever you want on TV. I've got to sort out Koa's gourmet lunch and let your soup cool a bit," I say, heading to the kitchen.

"Koa's getting the royal treatment too?" she asks.

"Of course. He's our fur baby, isn't he? Deserves all the love and chicken in the world." I tease.

Her laughter is like music, and I find myself smiling. Cooking wasn't in my playbook today, but seeing Ava like this, I'd whip up a feast any day.

―

AVA

Finishing off the last of Nick's culinary masterpiece – seriously, this soup could win awards – we're sprawled on the couch, 'Friends' playing in the background, *as always*. It's probably my millionth time watching it, but who's counting? It's like a warm, comforting blanket on a cold day.

Nick's arm is my personal snuggle fortress, wrapped around me as I burrow into the blanket. His heartbeat is a steady rhythm against my back, and his warmth is a soothing balm. I snuggle closer, feeling safe.

I steal a glance at Nick, the TV light casting a soft glow on his ruggedly handsome face. In this moment, wrapped in his embrace, it feels like I've found my own little slice of heaven.

As the credits roll, Nick shifts, his expression turning serious. "Ava," he starts.

I turn to face him, my heart thudding. "Yeah?"

He takes a deep breath, his eyes locking with mine in a gaze that pierces my soul. "I just wanted you to know that I love you." His voice is a soft murmur.

My heart leaps into my throat. "I love you too," I whisper back, my voice trembling.

His smile is like the sun breaking through the clouds, "I've never felt anything like this before. You're my first love, the real deal."

I lean into him, lost in the depth of his eyes. Without thinking, I close the distance between us, and our kiss is a tempest, as if we're trying to pour every unsaid word, every unexpressed feeling into this one moment.

We break apart and Nick looks at me. "I'm in this for the long run. I'm all in."

My lips part in total shock. "Oh my God, Nick!" My heart's racing like it's in the Indy 500.

"What?"

"I just kissed you!" I exclaim.

Nick chuckles, casually checking my forehead. "Yeah, love, it's not our first rodeo. You sure you're not feverish again?" he teases.

"No, I mean yes, I don't know!" I stammer. "I'm sorry! What if you catch this bug too?"

"It's worth the risk," he cuts in, planting another kiss on me, as casual as if he's flipping a coin.

I pull back, cheeks blazing. "No, Nick, I don't want you getting sick because of me."

He laughs, his eyes dancing with mischief. "Getting sick just means more time with you. Win-win."

"But I don't want you ill," I pout, feeling guilty.

"I'm tough," he reassures me with a confident grin.

"Tougher than this bug?"

"You're brutal with your words, sunshine." He teases. But then, the playfulness in his eyes shifts to something deeper. "Ava, I gotta set something straight," he says.

"What's that?" I ask, my heart skipping a beat.

He takes a deep breath, "From now on, if anyone asks, or even if they don't, I'm telling the world you're my girlfriend."

My heart races. "Are you — are you asking me to be your girlfriend?" I stammer.

He shakes his head, a smirk on his lips. "No, Ava. I'm not asking. You're already mine. Can't just kiss a guy like me and think you can walk away free."

"Guess that's how it's going to be then," I reply, my eyes locked with his.

And just like that, I – Ava Adams – find myself officially and irrevocably Nick Thompson's girlfriend.

Fever be damned, I slide onto Nick's lap, facing him, my hands cupping his face. Without a second thought, I plant another kiss on his lips.

Nick looks at me, his eyebrows raised. "What's all this for, sunshine?"

"Well, since I'm officially your girlfriend, might as well enjoy all the perks."

He smirks, his gaze intense and fixed on me as I daringly shed my pajama top, leaving nothing underneath. I catch Nick's eyes trailing a path down to my chest, then slowly moving back up to meet mine. He's doing this casual, oh-so-Nick bite on his bottom lip.

I don't give him a chance to even catch his breath. Diving in, I kiss him again, my lips meeting his with a fiery urgency. He responds, his hands finding the bare skin of my back, his touch sending a thrilling shiver across my skin.

Breaking the kiss, I start peeling his shirt off, but he's two steps ahead of me. In a smooth move, he shrugs it off himself, then pulls me back in, his kiss fierce and full of heat. I can feel him, hard and wanting, pressing against me through his trousers.

I run my fingers through his hair, tugging gently, eliciting a low growl from the back of his throat that sends waves down my spine.

"Easy there, tiger," I murmur against his lips, a playful glint in my eyes.

Nick's hands roam with a boldness that matches the fire in his eyes. "I can't help it," he whispers, his voice husky. "You're intoxicating, sunshine."

I find the hem of his trousers, my fingers teasing the waistband. His breath hitches, a clear sign that I've hit the mark.

"Looks like someone's enjoying the perks too," I quip, unable to resist the opportunity to tease him.

He chuckles, a sound that vibrates against my chest. "Guilty as charged," he admits, his eyes never leaving mine. But then, his expression turns serious, a depth in his gaze. "Ava," he starts, "I want you, all of you."

My heart pounds in response, "Then take me."

Without another word, Nick lifts me effortlessly, carrying me to the bedroom with a determination that leaves no room for doubt, and he lays me down gently.

"I've wanted this," his voice is a low rumble. "Wanted you like this."

I reach up, my hands framing his face. "Then what are you waiting for?"

Nick turns the heat up, his lips blazing a trail from mine down to my belly. He navigates a path across my chest, each kiss sending sparks through my veins. My breath hitches as he tugs my pants down to my ankles.

When he gets to the waistband of my panties, he pauses. There's a mischievous glint in his eyes as he kisses me, tossing my pants aside like they're nothing more than an afterthought.

He draws me closer, his strong hands guiding my legs as his lips find the fabric of my panties.

The room is filled with soft sighs, and the urgent rustle of fabric. We're lost in each other – in the storm we've created together.

CHAPTER SEVENTEEN

NICK

So, I caught the bug too, just like Ava predicted. But let's be honest, it was the perfect excuse to play hooky, stay in, and get cozy with her.

And by cozy, I mean... *well, you know.*

But, we're both on the mend now, thanks to some solid R&R and meds.

Now, here's the kicker — my parents are heading back to London tomorrow. And I've got this wild idea that they need to meet Ava before they jet off.

Yeah, never thought I'd be the guy wanting to do the meet-the-parents dance.

Tonight, it's farewell dinner time with Ella. Since Ava waltzed into my life, I've been aiming to step up my game — not just for her, but for myself and my family too. *Time to mend some bridges.*

The plan to introduce Ava to the family? Top secret. Only she's in on it. And, man, she's getting ready, looking like a dream in this light blue dress that fits her like a glove, white stilettos shining, and her hair doing this sexy, bouncy thing.

She's fiddling with her earrings, catching my eye in the mirror. "I'm nervous," she confesses.

"Love, it's me who should be sweating bullets here," I tell her, trying to ease her mind.

"But you're just being... you," she says.

"And what's that supposed to mean?"

"It means you look cool as a cucumber, and I'm here looking like a jittery mess," she says, finally turning to face me, all dolled up.

"You're not just stunning, Ava. You're breathtaking," I assure her, my eyes taking in every detail.

She gives me this shy smile, walking over and planting a soft one on my lips. "Thanks," her voice a soft melody.

"Ready to go show off to the family?"

"Show off? What, am I your latest trophy now?" she shoots back, feigning indignation.

"You're more than that. You're my masterpiece," I flirt, and her laughter fills the room, music to my ears.

"Nick, that's probably your best line yet," she says, still giggling.

I just grin, basking in her laughter. She's got this way of making even the most nerve-wracking plans feel like the best idea ever.

—

I pull up at Ella's house. Ava's sitting, a bundle of nerves, so I place my hand reassuringly on her thigh. "Relax, love. They're going to adore you."

"But what if they don't?"

I flash her a confident smile. "Ava, trust me, there's nothing to not like about you. You're incredible. And just so you know, two people in there already think the world of you."

"Two?" she echoes.

"Yes, me and Maggie," I remind her, hoping to ease her nerves.

Her face lights up at the mention of Maggie. "Right! Maggie will be there!"

"She's your biggest fan!"

Ava takes a deep breath. "Okay, I got this..."

"You absolutely do. We're in this together."

Stepping out, she hesitates. "Are you sure surprising them is a good idea?"

"We're about to find out," I say with a hint of mischief.

Ella opens the door, her face a perfect picture of shock, but not in a bad way. It takes her a moment to find her words. "Hi! I'm Ella!"

Ava, ever the charmer, beams back. "Hi! I'm Ava!" She's radiant, and Ella's still looking at me for answers.

"I'll fill you in soon," I promise Ella with a wink, leading Ava inside hand in hand.

"AVA!" Maggie's voice rings out, and she barrels into Ava, hugging her with all her might.

Ava, laughing, bends down to hug Maggie back. "Hey, pumpkin!"

Then Mum and Dad appear, and Mum's expression is something else. Shocked doesn't even begin to cover it.

"Hey, Mum," I greet, nudging Ava to stand beside me.

Mum moves in for a hug, then turns to Ava. "You look absolutely gorgeous, my dear."

Ava blushes, "Thank you. I'm Ava!"

"I know, darling. Maggie's told us so much about you," Mum replies, her eyes softening as she looks at Ava.

I give Ava a reassuring smile. "Told you about your number one fan."

Dad joins in, hugging me and giving Ava a warm welcome, his eyes shooting me a silent question.

"Okay," I say, gesturing for Ella to join us. Everyone gathers around, Maggie included.

I take a deep breath, holding Ava's hand. "This is Ava. I didn't plan on springing this on you, but I knew you'd be cool with it." I glance at Mum, who's already getting teary. "Yes, Mum, Ava's my girlfriend. But let's not scare her off, okay? Took me a while to find her."

Laughter fills the room, and I look at Ava, feeling like I've hit the jackpot.

EPILOGUE

Surveying the dining table, a wave of warmth crashes over me.

This is it – my world in one room. My parents, Ella, little Maggie, and then there's Ava, a vision across the table, her glow outshining the candlelight. I can't help but think how much Josh would have loved her.

Dinner wraps up, and a surge of anxiety hits me.

It's now or never.

I push back from the table, heart hammering. "I need to say something," I announce, every pair of eyes in the room swiveling to me.

Ava's clearly confused as I stride over to her, taking her hand, feeling its warmth and the slight tremble. "Ava," I start, "Since the day I met you, you've turned my world upside down – in the best way. It's been a year, and every day with you is a day worth living."

I can feel my pulse in my throat. There's no turning back now.

"Ava," I continue, dropping to one knee, my hand fishing out the small box I've been guarding all evening. "Will you make me the happiest man alive and marry me?"

Her eyes go wide, shimmering with tears. "Yes," she breathes, her voice a feather.

Ella lets out a delighted squeal, wrapping us in a hug all excited. "This is incredible!"

Mum's eyes are misty as she joins in, her embrace enveloping us. "I knew it. You two are perfect for each other."

Dad gives me a proud pat on the back, then turns to Ava with a tender smile. "Welcome to the family, my dear."

Ava's eyes, glistening with tears, meet mine. "Nick, I love you," she says, her voice quivering. "I can't wait for all our tomorrows."

I pull her in for a kiss, a promise sealed between us. In this moment, surrounded by love, I know we're just at the beginning of our forever.

This is more than a proposal – it's the start of a lifetime with the woman who's become my everything.

—

AVA

As I sit here, still reeling from the proposal, I notice the joy radiating from Nick's parents. Ella, with her infectious grin, seems as thrilled as if she herself just got engaged. And then it hits me – *I'm actually going to marry Nicholas Thompson.*

My gaze drifts to Maggie, who's blissfully playing with Koa, completely oblivious to the life-altering event that just unfolded. Her innocence in this moment is heartwarming.

Nick leans in, his breath tickling my ear. "Looks like Maggie's the only one not on the congratulatory bandwagon yet."

I chuckle, turning to him. "She's got her priorities. Koa first."

He plants a soft kiss on my cheek. "I'm so happy, Ava. So incredibly happy." He then takes my hand, "I still can't believe you said yes."

I smile, "I can't believe I get to spend my life with the most incredible man I've ever known."

His chuckle is low and warm. "Keep the compliments coming, Ms. Adams," he teases. "I always knew you were the one, Ava. I just never found the right words."

I turn to face him, my hand reaching up to caress his cheek. "You don't need words, Nick. You show me every single day."

He leans in, his kiss soft. "I love you, Ava Adams," he murmurs against my lips.

"And I love you, Nicholas Thompson."

In his arms I realize just how incredibly lucky I am.

Nicholas Thompson, the man who's stolen my heart, is now my fiancé.

Soon enough I'll be Ms. Thompson.

Ava Adams Thompson.

And here, lost in our own little world, I know that this is just the beginning of our forever.

ACKNOWLEDGMENTS

And so, we arrive at the acknowledgments of the refreshed edition of "This Little Thing Called Love." Pinch me, because I'm still trying to wrap my head around the fact that this dream continues! The journey of bringing this story back to life has been nothing short of surreal.

I must start with the biggest, warmest, and most heartfelt thank you to my incredible mom – **MY SUPERHERO WITHOUT A CAPE**. She's been the first to plunge into the deep end with me, from scrutinizing every detail of the cover to dissecting the character sketches and draft manuscripts. Her steadfast support and faith in my sometimes crazy, always ambitious endeavors have been my guiding light.

To my boyfriend, **MY ROCK-SOLID ANCHOR AND EVER-ENTHUSIASTIC PARTNER-IN-CRIME**, you deserve a galaxy of medals. He's been right there with me, through every word typed and every sentence deleted, offering insights that were pure gold. Your patience with my creative chaos and your unwavering belief in my vision have been invaluable.

Now, a little pat on the back for myself – **YES, IT'S TIME FOR SOME SELF-RECOGNITION**! Balancing a day job and burning the midnight oil to write was a Herculean task. But here we are, living proof that dreams do come true with persistence and passion.

And to the heartbeat of this adventure – **MY BOOKSTAGRAM FAMILY**. Your energy, enthusiasm, and engagement have been the wind beneath the wings of this book. To every reader, reviewer, and friend who's joined this journey, you form the pulse of this vibrant community. Your encouragement is the fuel that keeps this dream soaring.

So, here's to the crazy ups and downs, the 'oops' moments, and the 'ah-ha' surprises. The road ahead? It's like an uncharted map of who-knows-what, and I'm absolutely jazzed to be navigating it with all of you. Let's dive into more love, laughs, and those 'did that just happen?' moments, shall we?

With all my love and gratitude,
FRANCES BLACKTHORN

ABOUT THE AUTHOR

Home is where the heart is, and for me, that's somewhere in the beautiful, diverse tapestry of EUROPE. I share this adventure with my boyfriend and our two furry little devils, who are as mischievous as they are adorable. It's a life filled with love, chaos, and endless inspiration.

Since I was a teenager, books have been my escape, my passion, and my best friends. I guess it was inevitable that I'd turn this lifelong love affair into a career. And here I am — a writer, living the dream one word at a time.

Coffee is my fuel. Seriously, I can't function without it. It's my magic potion that helps me conjure up all those words and stories.

When I'm not glued to my computer, weaving new tales, you can find me curled up watching horror movies. Yep, I love a good scare! But, I also have a soft spot for the dark, whimsical worlds created by the genius Tim Burton. His films are my guilty pleasures — they're like eerie fairy tales for grown-ups.

So, that's a little snapshot of me. A bookworm-turned-author, living a life filled with stories, coffee, a touch of sarcasm, and a whole lot of love.

THANKS FOR JOINING ME ON THIS JOURNEY.